PRAISE FOR
MEET ME AT THE MORGUE

and
Ross Macdonald

"All the pace and excitement of earlier Macdonalds. . . . A legitimately surprising solution."
—*New York Times*

❋

"Characters in the round, believable evil and clarity of telling make another fine Macdonald story."
—*San Francisco Chronicle*

❋

"Ross Macdonald gives to the detective story that accent of class that the late Raymond Chandler did."
—**Seymour Korman,** *Chicago Tribune*

❋

"Macdonald should not be limited in audience to connoisseurs of mystery fiction. He is one of a handful of writers in the genre whose worth and quality surpass the limitations of the form."
—**Robert Kirsch,** *Los Angeles Times*

❋

more . . .

"It was not just that Ross Macdonald taught us how to write; he did something much more, he taught us how to read, and how to think about life, and maybe in some small, but mattering way, how to live. . . . I owe him."
—**Robert B. Parker**

✳

"Let's be honest: Ross Macdonald remains *the* grandmaster, taking the crime novel to new heights by imbuing it with psychological resonance, complexity of story, and richness of style that remain awe-inspiring. Those of us in his wake owe a debt that can never be paid."
—**Jonathan Kellerman**

✳

"Ross Macdonald is an important American novelist."
—*San Francisco Chronicle*

✳

"Most mystery writers merely write about crime. Ross Macdonald writes about sin."
—*Atlantic*

✳

"[Ross Macdonald] carried form and style about as far as they would go, writing classic family tragedies in the guise of private detective mysteries."
—*The Guardian*

✳

ALSO BY ROSS MACDONALD

The Barbarous Coast
Black Money
The Moving Target
The Chill
The Galton Case
The Blue Hammer
The Way Some People Die
The Far Side of the Dollar
The Wycherly Woman
The Doomsters
The Ferguson Affair
The Three Roads

Published by
WARNER BOOKS

ROSS MACDONALD

MEET ME AT THE MORGUE

WARNER BOOKS

A Time Warner Company

WARNER BOOKS EDITION

This Warner Books Edition is published by arrangement with
Alfred A. Knopf, Inc., 201 East 50th Street, New York, N.Y. 10022.

Cover design by Jackie Merri Meyer
Cover illustration by Gary Kelley

Warner Books, Inc.
666 Fifth Avenue
New York, N.Y. 10103

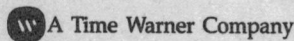 A Time Warner Company

Printed in the United States of America

First Warner Books Printing: March, 1991

10 9 8 7 6 5 4 3 2 1

To my favorite in-laws
Dorothy & Clarence

CAST OF CHARACTERS

CHAPTER
1

I met the boy on the morning of the kidnapping. It was a bright and blowing day. The wind was fresh from the sea, and the piled white cubes of the city sparkled under a swept blue sky. I had to force myself to go to work.

A bronze-painted sports car with a long foreign nose was standing at the curb in front of the County Annex building. I parked in my regular space, a few yards behind it. So far as I knew, there was only one bronze Jaguar in town. It belonged to Abel Johnson. I wasn't surprised when Fred Miner, Johnson's driver, emerged from my second-floor office and started down the outside steps to the street.

Fred reached the sidewalk and turned in my direction, a stocky man in his middle thirties who walked with a peculiar stiff-backed roll. The faded Navy suntans he always wore had darker patches on the sleeve, where his Chief's stripes and hash-mark had been removed. His only concession to his civilian occupation was a black, peaked chauffeur's cap, which shadowed his eyes. He passed my car without seeing me, his face closed in thought.

There was a yelp and a flurry of movement from the sports car. A small boy with a head a bright red hair scrambled over the door and launched himself like a missile at Fred's legs. The man's face opened in a laugh of pure delight. Taking the boy under the arms, he swung him upside down in the air and set him back on his feet:

"Knock it off now, swabbie. This is no time for games. Come to attention."

"Okay, Fred," the boy chirped. "Aye, aye, sir, I mean." He brought his feet together and arched his back.

"Now wipe that smile off your face or I'll break you down to apprentice seaman and take away your privileges for fifteen years."

"Aye, aye, sir."

The boy giggled. Fred tried to repress a snort of mirth, and couldn't. They stood on the sidewalk laughing into each other's face. Passers-by smiled at them.

I stepped out of my car. When Fred saw me his face changed. "Morning, Mr. Cross," he said without enthusiasm.

"Hell, Fred. Looking for me?"

"I came in to see Mr. Linebarge."

"He's on his vacation."

"Yeah, the little lady told me. I was up to your office already."

"I thought you didn't have to report until next week."

"It wasn't that. I didn't come in to report. It was just a couple of questions I wanted to take up with Mr. Linebarge."

"About your probation?"

He looked sheepish, and shifted his weight from one leg to the other and back again. Being on probation embarrassed Fred. "More or less. It wasn't anything important."

"Can I help?"

He backed away a step. "No, I wouldn't want to bother you, Mr. Cross. I'll be seeing Mr. Linebarge next Saturday, anyway. He'll be back next Saturday, won't he?"

"He will if he doesn't drown. He's gone on a fishing-trip."

The boy reached up and tugged at Fred's belt. "Is something the matter? Can't we go on our trip?"

"Sure we can, Jamie," He brushed the cropped red head with his hand. "Remember now, no talking in the ranks."

"Is this the Johnson boy?" I said.

"Yessir, this is Jamie Johnson. Jamie, meet Mr. Cross." He added with a trace of irony: "Mr. Cross is a very good friend of mine."

The boy gave me a sticky hand. "Pleased to meet you, Mr. Cross. Any friend of Fred's is a friend of mine."

Fred's face lit up, but he said in a quarterdeck voice: "You hustle back aboard now, before you talk yourself to death."

The boy scampered back to the Jaguar and dove head first over the low door. The last I was of him was a thin denim behind and a pair of kicking moccasins.

"He's a bright youngster," I said. "How old is he?"

"Watch it, he'll hear you." Fred crossed his lips with an oil-grained forefinger, and lowered his voice. "He shouldn't hear himself praised too much, it might give him a swell head. It's going to be tough enough on him with all the dough in the family. Jamie's four."

"He's doing all right for four. Who taught him his manners?"

"He'll get by. I make him toe the mark." Fred started to move away. "Well, so long, Mr. Cross. Nice seeing you."

"Hold it a minute. What's up?"

"There's nothing up," he answered woodenly.

"The boy said you were going on a trip. You're not leaving the county?"

"No, I'm not going anywhere." He was a long time answering.

I was almost sure he was lying. "You know the rules. You're not allowed to go out of the county without definite permission from our office."

"I know it." He colored uncomfortably. "I'm just taking Jamie for a ride. Is that illegal?"

"You're not supposed to drive except in line of work."

"I got my orders. That makes it work, doesn't it?" He glanced nervously towards the sports car. "I ought to be on my way now, Mr. Cross."

"Your way to where?"

His face had closed up completely again, into a mask of blank hostility. "I'm not supposed to tell anybody that."

"Are you in some kind of trouble?"

"No sir, I'm not. I haven't been in any trouble since February and I don't intend to get into any trouble." He said it with conviction.

"I'll take your word for it, Fred. You're all right as long as you don't leave the county, obey the traffic laws, and stay on the wagon. You know what happens if you break those conditions."

From the courthouse tower across the street, a bell began to sound the three-quarter hour. We both looked up at the tower clock. It was a quarter to nine.

"I know what happens," he said. "I've got to shove off now, Mr. Cross."

"What's the hurry?"

He didn't answer. The vibration of the bell still hung in the air above us like an echoing warning. He squinted up at the great iron-faced clock and shifted his feet impatiently.

"That's a fast car," I said. "What will it do?"

"A hundred and twenty, maybe. I never opened her up."

"Remember to hold it down to fifty-five."

"I'll remember. Can I go now?"

I watched him climb into the driver's seat of the Jaguar. It was a tight fit. Fred was thick in the chest and wide across the shoulders, and his back was stiff from being broken in the war. As he was maneuvering himself in under the low convertible top, I noticed the gun-shaped bulge in his hip pocket.

I wasn't sure it was a gun. I didn't know whether he had the legal right to carry one. Before I decided to stop him, the bronze car leaped away from the curb and disappeared around the corner of the courthouse. The fading sound of its motor was like an ill wind.

Ann Devon looked up from her typewriter when I entered the outer office. She was one of my two assistant probation-officers, a mouse blonde with a recent degree in psychology and large untapped reserves of girlish fervor. Turned in her chair against the light from the window, she made a very pleasant silhouette.

"Good morning, 'Howie. There's something on your mind."

"Please don't be intuitive so early in the day. I find it wearing."

"You might as well tell me," she said. "You always get those nasty vertical wrinkles between the eyebrows."

"Maybe it wasn't such a bad idea."

"What wasn't?"

"Burning witches."

"Come on now, Howie. Tell good gray Doctor Devon." She was twenty-four.

I sat on the corner of her desk. On the far corner she had set a bowl of multicolored sweet peas that contrasted prettily with the calcimined walls and scuffed office furniture.

"What was Fred Miner after, or wouldn't he tell you, either?"

"He wanted to see Alex. I told him Alex was away, and he seemed rather worried and disappointed."

"Did he say why?"

"He mumbled something obscure about wanting to go through channels, and do the right thing for everybody."

"I think there's something up his sleeve," I said. "I met him on the sidewalk just now, and he acted pretty evasive. I couldn't get him to open up."

"You won't be mad if I tell you something, Howie? I think he's afraid of you."

"Of me?"

"Quite a few people are. When you put on that grim righteous look. I was scared myself for the first six months or so."

"I don't see why."

"You have a terrible lot of power over these people."

"I don't misuse it if I can help it." The conversation was beginning to irritate me.

"I know you don't. I wonder if Fred Miner knows it, though. With his Navy experience, he must be aware of what official power can do to him if he makes the slightest slip. After all, he doesn't know you the way he does Alex. I told him you'd be in soon, but he wouldn't wait. Probably he came in to ask Alex's advice about some private problem."

"He didn't say anything about going away?"

"Not a word. I'm sure you don't have to be concerned about him. Alex told me he's adjusting wonderfully." Ann's blue eyes darkened with feeling. "Personally I think he's a sturdy character. If I killed a man with my car, I swear I'd never be able to drive again."

"You call it driving, what you do?"

"I'm serious. You mustn't make fun of me."

"You mustn't waste all your fine emotion on a hit-run driver and a married man to boot."

She colored slightly. "Don't be ridiculous. My feelings about our clients are quite impersonal. Anyway, he isn't a hit-run driver, morally speaking. Alex says he didn't know he'd run over anyone, so it wasn't his fault."

"When they've been drinking, it's always their fault. You can pin that in your hat. It's an axiom."

Her eyes widened. "Had he been drinking? Alex didn't tell me that."

"Alex doesn't talk about his cases any more than he has to. It's a good rule to follow."

She said with a flash of impudence: "You're very moral-lecturey this morning." But her curiosity overcame her pique. "How do you know Fred Miner was drinking that night?"

"I read the police report. They gave him an intoximeter test when they arrested him. He was heavily loaded, over two hundred milligrams."

"Poor man. I didn't realize he was that way. Perhaps we

should run a Rorschach on him. Alcoholics always have deep-seated emotional problems—''

"He isn't alcoholic. He simply got drunk, as a lot of people do, and killed a man. Don't waste your sympathy on him, because he's been lucky. His wife stayed with him. His boss stood by him. If it wasn't for that, and his war record, Miner would be in jail.''

"Well, I'm glad he isn't.'' She added irrationally: "Even if you're not.''

She lowered her head and fired a machine-gun burst on the typewriter. Our conversation often ended like that. I liked to think that it was the ancient conflict between heart and head, with me representing head.

The courthouse clock had already struck nine, and I felt its delayed, guilty echo. Closing the door of the inner office rather sharply, I took off my jacket for work and spent the next two hours on the dictaphone. I was doing a report on a prosperous matron who had been arrested for stealing several dresses from local shops. The dresses were invariably size nine. The lady was size eighteen, and had no children.

Between the paragraphs, my mind kept turning to Fred Miner. Though I wouldn't admit it to Ann, I felt a certain satisfaction in his case. Three months ago, in early February, it hadn't looked too promising.

According to the sheriff's office and the city police, Fred had got himself violently drunk on a Saturday night, had taken one of his employer's cars without permission, had run a man down in the road near Johnson's country house, and then driven on into town without stopping. The city police caught him steering in long sweeping arcs along the ocean boulevard, and booked him for drunken driving. The sheriff's men didn't find the body in the road until later that night, and then they were unable to identify the victim.

But one of the fog lamps was smashed on the Lincoln that Fred had been driving. Fragments of yellow glass from the fog lamp were scattered at the scene of the accident. One long shard of glass was found imbedded in the dead man's eye cavity.

The courthouse crowd predicted that Fred would be found guilty on a felony charge and sentenced to two to five years in state prison. Then Abel Johnson came back from his winter house in the desert. He found bail for Fred and put his personal lawyer on the case. The lawyer, a man named Seifel, pleaded him guilty to a reduced charge of involuntary manslaughter and applied for probation.

I assigned Alex Linebarge to do the report on Miner. Alex spent nearly a month going over his record with a fine-tooth comb. He came up with the conclusion that Fred Miner was a solid citizen who had made one grave mistake but wasn't very likely to make another. Fred was sentenced to one year in the county jail, suspended; he was fined three hundred dollars and put on five years' probation.

On the whole he had been lucky, as I said. His life had been salvaged, and my department had a stake in it. He'd fallen, been caught before he hit the bottom, and hoisted back the moral tightrope that everyone has to walk every day.

But a man on probation walks on his own high wire without a net. If he falls twice, he falls hard, into prison.

CHAPTER
2

A burst of voices from the outer office broke into my thoughts. I switched off the dictaphone. One of the voices was Ann's. She seemed to be trying to quiet another voice, which rose and fell in surges of emotion. One of her juvenile clients, I thought, having a tantrum or a crying spell.

When I thought that it had lasted long enough, I opened the pebbled glass door. A woman who was far from juvenile was slumped in the interview chair beside Ann's desk. Under a cheap, print house-dress, her body was long and angular. Ann was bent over her with one hand on her gaunt shoulder.

I recognized her when she lifted her face in the light. She seemed to have aged ten years in the three months since I had seen her. There were strands of gray like steel shavings caught in her straight brown hair. Her eyes were red-rimmed and her mouth was distraught.

"What's the trouble, Mrs. Miner?"

"Terrible trouble." With difficulty, she controlled the trembling of her lips. "It came down on me out of a blue sky."

I looked at Ann.

"I don't quite know what she means," she said. "It's something about a kidnapping. Mrs. Miner is afraid her husband is involved in some way."

"No!" the woman cried. "It isn't true. Fred couldn't do a thing like that. He couldn't, I ought to know. We've been married for ten years, and Fred is the kindest man. He loves that boy."

I crossed the room and stood over her. "Has the Johnson boy been kidnapped?"

She raised her wet black lashes. "Yes, and they're accusing Fred. They claim he stole the boy and ran away with him. But it's a lie." Her voice broke in a storm of grief.

"Mrs. Miner says there's a plot against him." Ann leaned towards me and added in a whisper: "Do you think she's having delusions of persecution?"

"Nonsense," I said, more loudly than I intended.

Mrs. Miner jerked herself upright, dislodging Ann's hand from her shoulder. "Don't you believe me? It's the truth

I'm telling you. Jamie's been stolen and Fred's been framed to take the blame for it.'' Under the thin flesh, her high cheekbones stood out as if grief had washed them bare.

"Take it easy," I said. "I can't believe you or disbelieve you until I've heard what happened. Bring her a drink of water, will you, Miss Devon?"

"Of course." Ann filled a paper cup at the earthenware cooler and brought it to Mrs. Miner. "There you are, dear."

With a shaking hand, she raised the cup to her pale unpainted lips. Some of the water spilled down the front of her dress. She gulped the rest of it and crushed the cup in her fist. Her knuckles were red and cracked from housework.

"Now tell Mr. Cross what you told me," Ann prompted her.

"I'll try." She made an effort to be calm. Above the square-cut collar of her dress, the cords in her neck bulged taut like thin ropes. "You saw my husband this morning? He said he was coming here to talk to Mr. Linebarge."

"He was here. Mr. Linebarge wasn't, but I talked to him."

"Did he look to you like he was planning a crime? Did he? Is that the way he looked?"

I felt a repetition of the qualms I had had that morning, talking to Fred. "Perhaps I'd better ask the questions, Mrs. Miner. You say your husband's been accused of kidnapping Jamie Johnson. Who accused him?"

"Mr. Johnson."

"On what grounds?"

"No ground at all. It's a plot." The stiff movement of her jaws gave her speech an oddly ventriloquial effect.

"You've said that. Can't you tell me anything more definite? I take it they're both gone."

"Both of them, vanished like smoke." One of her hands flipped up in an involuntary gesture. She returned it, clenched to her lap. "It doesn't mean Fred is guilty. It means the opposite. It means foul play."

"Nobody knows where they are?"

"Somebody knows. I don't, but somebody knows. Who- ever it is behind all this, they know." Her mouth was tight and hissing. Her eyes glared like brown glass.

"Who do you have in mind?"

"A conspiracy," she said, "that's what it is."

Ann and I looked at each other. I was half inclined to agree with her that Mrs. Miner had been unbalanced by the shock of events.

"He's got a big black mark against him," she was saying, "and *they* know that. It's a criminal conspiracy to put the blame on him, for stealing the child."

"Has Jamie really been kidnapped?"

"I'm telling the truth," she said fiercely. "What do you think?"

"I think you may be exaggerating a little." I looked at my wristwatch. "It's twenty to twelve now. I saw the boy with Fred less than three hours ago. There was no trouble then."

She leaned towards me, her thin face avid for any kind of hope. "I knew it. Fred loved the boy like his own son. I knew there couldn't be trouble between them, only Mr. Johnson won't take my word for it. He's blaming Fred. They're all down on him now, even Mr. Johnson. He said he made a terrible mistake when he saved Fred from going to prison."

Ann said in surprise: "Does Mr. Johnson think his son has been kidnapped?"

"He knows it."

"How can he know it?" I said. "The boy's only been gone since nine o'clock. Fred told me he had orders to take him for a drive."

"I don't know about that." The authority of special information had restored some of her self-control. "All I know is, I saw the ransom letter with my own eyes. It came in the mail this morning. I took it up to the main house myself. I was there when Mr. Johnson opened it."

Ann and I looked at each other in silence. The first stroke

of the three-quarter-hour fell from the courthouse tower like a bomb of sound, a giant exclamation-mark at the end of the woman's statement. Between the first stroke and the third the situation changed palpably. Even the familiar room altered in appearance.

I echoed stupidly: "A ransom letter?"

"Yes. It came in the mail this morning."

"Did it mention Fred?"

"Of course it didn't. He's got nothing to do with this, can't you believe me? It gave instructions like for paying the money. It wasn't even signed."

"How much, Mrs. Miner?"

"Fifty thousand dollars."

Ann whistled. Fifty thousand dollars would pay her salary for nearly twenty years, and mine for nearly ten.

"He called the police, I hope."

"No. He didn't. He was afraid to. The letter said if he did they'd kill the boy."

"Where's Johnson now?"

"He came into town to raise the money. I haven't seen him since he left the house. He was in an awful rush. The letter only gave him till eleven o'clock."

"You mean the money's been paid already?"

"I guess so. He was going to pay it all right. He dotes on that boy." She added defensively: "No more than Fred, though."

"I know that. Tell me this. Have you any idea where Fred is?"

"I only wish I had. He didn't tell me, except about Mr. Linebarge. He said he was coming here, and that's all."

"Did he say why?"

"Not him. He kept things to himself."

"Do you know if he took the boy without permission?"

"That's what Mr. Johnson says. Fred never did it before. Fred always tried to do the right thing."

Ann said: "Is Mrs. Johnson out there alone?"

"As far as I know she is. She's taking it calm enough, or

I wouldn't have left her. When they started making these accusations, I had to come in and see—"

I interrupted her: "We'd better go out there. Do you have a car, Mrs. Miner?"

"We had. Fred had to sell it to pay his fine. I rode in on the bus."

"I'll drive you out."

"Shouldn't we call the Federal Bureau?" Ann said.

"Not without talking to Johnson first. It's his boy."

CHAPTER
3

I knew Abel Johnson slightly. He had come into the office in February to discuss the Miner case, and Alex had introduced us. Johnson was an expansive middle-aged man who was supposed to have made a moderate fortune in San Diego real estate during the war. A year or so after the war ended he retired to Pacific Point and bought a country house a few miles out of town. There he settled down with his wife and baby son.

The courthouse gossip said that he had been seriously ill and had married his nurse. I had never met Mrs. Johnson. Johnson himself was regarded as a leading citizen. He was a heavy contributor to local charities and a member of the retired executives' club. If his son had really been kidnapped, there was going to be a great deal of strong public feeling.

Mrs. Miner acted as if she knew that. She hung back at the foot of the Annex stairs, watching the Saturday noon crowd with a kind of terror. Ann Devon had to coax her across the sidewalk and into my car. She walked stumbling, with her head bowed, like someone carrying a heavy burden. Once in the car, she shrank into a corner of the back seat and covered her eyes with her hand as if the sunlight hurt them. As we drove out of town, I heard her crying quietly to herself.

Pacific Point lay on the coastal slope at the ocean's edge. Driving up the terraced ridge of foothills behind the town, I could see the curved spit of land which had given the city its name, half enclosing the oval blue lagoon. The harbor and the sea beyond it were flecked with sails.

The road gained the crest of the ridge and curved along it briefly. Far ahead and to my left, Catalina floated like a shadowy dreadnought on the northwest horizon. Below and to my right, a dark green inland sea of orange groves flowed calm between the foothills and the mountains. It was a bright May day, but the colors of the country failed to lift me. They only emphasized the strangeness of our errand.

A black-top road branched off to the right. A black and white wooden sign at the fork announced: PACIFIC POINT CITY LIMITS. POPULATION 34,197. ELEVATION 21. There was a yellow Bus Stop sign beside it.

The woman in the back seat said in a muffled voice: "You turn off here."

I turned. Ann, who was riding beside me, touched my arm significantly. "This is where it happened," she whispered. "They found the body here, just below the crossroads."

Even in full daylight, it was a lonely place. Though I knew there were houses within earshot, they were the hidden houses of the rich. The road was masked on both sides by high laurel hedges and overarched by eucalyptus trees whose fallen leaves crackled under the wheels. I caught a glimpse of Mrs. Miner's face in the rear-view mirror. There was remembered horror on it. She might have just seen the dead man in the road.

A couple of miles further on, she said: "You better slow down, Mr. Cross. It's a sharp turn into the drive."

I did as she suggested, and turned between stone gate-posts onto fresh gravel. A weathering stone gatehouse stood behind a planting of Monterey cypress. Its small geometric garden was vivid with flowers.

Ann turned to speak to Mrs. Miner: "Do you want to get out here? Isn't this where you live?"

"I guess not after today. We'll be out in the street."

"You'd better come along with us," I said. "You know Mrs. Johnson and I don't."

"All right."

"Are you employed by the Johnsons?" Ann asked her.

"Not regular. She don't—she doesn't like regular servants around the house, she's very independent. I help her with the cleaning, though. And when she throws a party I always pitch in."

The main house stood a few hundred feet below the gatehouse, near the edge of a ravine. It was a flat-roofed structure of redwood and stone, built around three sides of a patio. I parked on the turnaround at the rear. There were two cars in the garages, and places for two others. One was the heavy black Lincoln sedan that had killed a man.

A red-haired woman in a green dress opened the back door and stepped out onto the small delivery-porch. She carried a light shotgun under her arm. When I was halfway out of the car, she leveled it at me. I got back in and let the door close itself.

Her voice rang out: "Who are you? What do you want?"

An echo from the hillside repeated the questions idiotically.

"I'm the County Probation Officer."

She called again over the steady gun: "What do you want?"

"To help you if I can."

"I don't need any help."

The woman in the back seat leaned forward to the window: "Mrs. Johnson! It's me. Mr. Cross drove me out."

The red-haired woman showed no enthusiasm. "Where do you think you've been?" But she lowered the gun.

Mrs. Miner poked me timidly between the shoulder blades. "Is it all right if I get out?"

"We all will." I was feeling a trifle let down. Johnson's wife had none of the earmarks of a damsel in distress. She handled a gun as if she knew how to use it.

On closer inspection, however, she showed her strain. Approaching her rather gingerly, I saw that her skin was bloodless, almost paper-white. Her eyes were opaque and too steady, like green stones. A tremor ran through her body spasmodically.

I looked to see that the safety was on the shotgun. It was. "Why the armament, Mrs. Johnson?"

"I didn't know who it was. I thought if *they* came—"

"The kidnappers?"

"Yes. I intended to kill them." She added quietly: "I only have the one child."

With her fiery hair and fair bold brow, her rather heavy lower lip pushed out, she looked capable of killing. She was like a young lioness robbed of her cub. She stood with her legs braced apart, holding the gun at waist level in front of her like a bar. Her body hadn't yet learned from her mind, or had forgotten, that we were friends.

"It's really true, then," Ann said.

"I told you," said Mrs. Miner.

The red-haired woman turned on her: "You weren't to call the police! Haven't you got it through your skull that Jamie's in danger?"

"I'm not the police," I said. "Mrs. Miner has been trying to trace her husband's movements. He came to our office this morning."

"Was Jamie with him?"

"Yes. As a matter of fact, he introduced me to Jamie. I'm no mind-reader, but he didn't act like a man planning a kidnapping."

Mrs. Miner gave me a grateful look.

"I'm not one to jump to conclusions," Mrs. Johnson said. "My husband did, I'm afraid—he's excitable. For myself, I won't believe that Fred Miner did such a thing to us. Not until I see the actual proof of it."

"Did you authorize him to take Jamie for a ride?"

"No. I didn't."

"He told me this morning that you had."

"No, I wasn't even up when they left. I took a pill last night. I don't usually sleep so late. Jamie didn't even have breakfast." The homely detail overcame her suddenly. Her eyes filled with tears.

Mrs. Miner laid a worn hand on her arm. "I gave him a banana and an orange. That was about eight o'clock, a little after. Fred drove him from the garage in the Jaguar. He told me he was going into town, that he had a matter to discuss with Mr. Linebarge. I naturally thought you gave him permission."

"I didn't. Neither did my husband." There was a frantic overtone in her voice.

Ann said briskly: "May we come in, Mrs. Johnson? I'd like to make you some coffee."

"You're very kind. Please come in." After its spasm of aggression, her body slumped wearily against the doorpost. I took the shotgun out of her hands before she dropped it, and set it in the corner behind the door.

"I'll make the coffee," Mrs. Miner said to Ann. "I know where everything is. She could probably use a bite to eat, too."

In the presence of the other woman's distress, Mrs. Miner had recovered her composure. She managed to give me a faint rueful smile as I passed her in the kitchen. Ann stayed in the kitchen with her.

CHAPTER
4

I followed Mrs. Johnson through the house into the central living-room. It was very large, perhaps twenty feet high and forty feet long. One entire wall was occupied by a semi-hexagonal window that overhung the ravine and revealed the valley beyond it.

She went to the window and stood with her back to me, looking out. Against the expanse of space, her figure seemed tiny and forlorn. It was a big country, and a four-year-old boy was a very small object to look for.

She said to herself, or to the distant, gray mountains: "It's a judgment on me. Everything has been easy and soft for me, since I married Abel. You pay for a little happiness in this life. I'd almost forgotten that. You pay for one thing with another."

I came up behind her, my footfalls soft on the rug. "I don't blame you for feeling fatalistic, Mrs. Johnson. I don't think you're right, though."

"What I said is true. I married money, I thought I was one of the lucky ones. I was. They single out the lucky ones for terrible blows like this. They'd have left us alone if we were poor. I wish I was poor again. I'd give everything I have." Her eyes ranged the lofty room, the paneled walls, the costly furniture. "Money is a curse, do you know it?"

"Not necessarily. Poor people have their bad times, too. I spend most of my working-time with poor people in trouble."

Her glance lighted on my face and stayed. The green eyes had cleared, and seemed to be seeing me for the first time. "Who did you say you were?"

"Howard Cross. I'm County Probation Officer."

"Abel's mentioned you, I think. Aren't you with the police?"

"I work with them, but under a different code. I'm a sort of middleman between the law and the lawbreaker."

"I don't think I understand you."

"I'll put it another way. The criminal is at war with society. Society fights back through cops and prisons. I try to act as neutral arbitrator. The only way to end the war is to make some kind of peace between the two sides."

"I'm not a service-club luncheon," she flared out. "Is that how you feel about this case? Neutral?"

"Hardly. There's no probation on a kidnapping conviction. It carries the death penalty, and I think it should. On the other hand, I feel as you do, it's dangerous to jump to conclusions. My office helped to keep Fred Miner out of jail, and I may be prejudiced. But I don't think he's the type. It takes a cruel mind to plan and execute a kidnapping."

"That's what's driving me crazy. I can't imagine what happened. Why would he take Jamie away like that, without even telling me?"

"I can't guess his reason, though I'm pretty sure he had a reason, or something that appeared to be a reason. Fred's not very bright, you know."

"He's not a genius. But he is goodhearted, and responsible. At least I've always believed that he was, in spite of his—accident." She ended on a vague and questioning note. "What is your opinion, Mr. Cross?"

"I have none." The possibilities that occurred to me, another accident, or foul play, would only add to her worry. "Whatever happened, we're wasting time. I think you should call the police."

"I'll show you why we haven't."

Moving quickly and rather blindly, she crossed the room

to a table in the corner and brought me a folded sheet of typewriter paper.

"The ransom note?"

She nodded. I unfolded the letter, which had been printed in block capitals with a pencil:

MISTER JOHNSON. WE HAVE YOUR BOY. NO HARM WILL COME TO HIM IF YOU OBEY ORDERS. FIRST NO CONTACT WITH POLICE REPEAT NO POLICE IF YOU WANT HIM BACK ALIVE. SECOND THE MONEY. FIFTY THOUSAND IN BILLS FIFTIES AND SMALLER. PURCHASE SMALL BLACK SUIT-CASE. PLACE MONEY IN SUITCASE. PLACE SUITCASE OUT-SIDE NEWS STAND AT PACIFIC POINT RAILWAY STATION BEHIND OUTSIDE NEWSPAPER RACK BETWEEN RACK AND WALL. THIS TO BE DONE BY YOU PERSONALLY AT 2 MINUTES TO 11 THIS SATURDAY MORNING. SAN DIEGO TRAIN LEAVES STATION AT 11:01. YOU LEAVE ON IT. ANY ATTEMPT TO SPY ON SUITCASE WILL BE FATAL TO BOY. TREAT US RIGHT WE TREAT HIM RIGHT WILL RE-TURN HIM TODAY.

"Miner didn't figure this out," I said.

"I know he didn't." She flung herself into a low square-cut chair. "The question is, who did. It reads to me like a letter from hell."

"A professional criminal or more likely a gang of them. It's very carefully cased and set up. The lettering was done with a ruler, to minimize handwriting characteristics. The whole things shows experience."

"You mean they've done this before, and got away with it?"

"I doubt that. Kidnapping's a pretty rare crime since the federal law was passed. Successful kidnappings are practically unheard of. I mean that you're dealing with hardened criminals. And I strongly urge you to call the police."

"I daren't. I promised Abel."

"Let me, then. The F.B.I. has the organization and equipment to find your son. Nobody else has. Jamie has a better chance of coming home safe with them than he has any other way. Why do you think they're so insistent about not bringing in the law?''

She shook her head rapidly. For a moment her face was a white blur under whirling red hair. ''I don't know. I can't make any decision. You mustn't ask me to. If Abel comes home and finds officers in the house, it might kill him.''

''Is he that vulnerable?''

''He's quite ill. The doctor expressly warned him about emotional shocks. You see, Abel had a coronary thrombosis in 1946. I didn't even want him to go to town this morning. But he was bound to do it himself.''

I looked at my watch: it was half past twelve. ''He'll be in San Diego by now, if he got that train.''

''No, Larry was going to follow the train in his car. It stops at Sapphire Beach, about ten miles down the line.''

''Larry?''

''Larry Seifel, my husband's lawyer. We got in touch with him right away.''

''He defended Miner on the hit-run charge, didn't he?''

''Yes.'' She shifted uneasily. ''I wonder what's keeping them. Abel said he'd be back by noon.''

I held the ransom letter up by one corner. ''Mrs. Miner told me this came in the morning mail. What time was that?''

''About half past nine. We were just sitting down to breakfast. I'd been calling Jamie, and got no answer. Jamie always wakes up so early. I'm afraid I fell into the habit of letting Fred look after him in the mornings.'' Guilt pulled at the corners of her mouth and made her grimace. ''They seemed to get along so well.''

I brought her back to the point: ''They didn't give your husband much time. From nine thirty to eleven is only an hour and a half. Where's the envelope, by the way?''

''The one that came in? I'll get it.''

She rose and fetched a plain white envelope from the table. It was addressed in the same square penciled letters to Mr. Abel Johnson, Valley Vista Ranch, Ridgecrest Road,

Pacific Point. The postmark was: Pacific Point, 6:51 P.M., May 9—the previous day.

The implications of the postmark struck me suddenly. The ransom letter had been composed and mailed at least fourteen hours before the actual kidnapping. Someone had been very sure of his timing.

"Excuse me." Leaving the letter and envelope on the table, I went back to the kitchen. At the table, Mrs. Miner was arranging a plate of sandwiches, and Ann was mixing salad in a wooden bowl.

"Where was your husband last night, Mrs. Miner?"

"I don't know. He went out. He had to drive the Johnsons into town."

"What time did he leave here?"

"I'm not sure. Some time after seven, it must have been. I gave him supper a while before he left."

Mrs. Johnson spoke from the doorway behind me: "It was seven fifteen. We had a dinner engagement, and I asked for the car at that time. Before that, he was in the patio all afternoon cleaning the pool. Jamie helped him. So he couldn't have mailed the letter. I thought of that."

"Who stayed with Jamie last night?"

"I did," said Mrs. Miner. "Poor lamb."

"And your dinner engagement, Mrs. Johnson?"

"It was with Larry Seifel and his mother. Why?"

Ann dropped a fork on the enameled steel tabletop. We all looked at her. She was blushing helplessly, for no reason I could see. Then wheels churned the gravel in the drive.

CHAPTER
5

There were pounding footsteps outside. Mrs. Johnson brushed
past me and ran to the open back door. A man's voice,
breathless and thin, cried: "Has he come back, Helen? Is he
here?"

"Not yet." She assume a cool professional tone. "You
know you shouldn't run, dear. Now come in and sit down
and be quiet."

"It's hard to hold myself back. I should be out looking
for him."

"No, Abel. There's a friend of yours here. Come in and
talk to him."

Johnson came through the back kitchen, his wife's solici-
tous arm around his shoulders. I had a queer twinge of pity,
or some other feeling, when I saw the two together: the
handsome fire-haired woman supporting the aging man. He
needed support. His white head, darkened with perspiration,
drooped on his shoulders. Hatless and coatless and unshaved,
he looked smaller and older than I remembered him.

As soon as he saw me and Ann, he straightened up and
pushed his wife away with a weak impatient gesture. I
suspected that he was drawing on his last reserves of energy.
"Cross? What brings you here? That courthouse grapevine
working overtime?"

"Mrs. Miner came to my office about an hour ago." I
explained why.

While I was talking, Larry Seifel came in behind him and paused in the doorway. Tall and young and broad-shouldered in a double-breasted gabardine suit that accentuated his build, he made a curious contrast with his employer. Mrs. Johnson's familiar glance at him seemed to take note of the contrast. Except that his eyes were a shade too sharp and bright in his tanned face, his square crew-cut a shade too consciously youthful, Larry Seifel was a very presentable young man.

A look of recognition passed between him and Ann Devon. Her blush was still burning like the glow from an inner fire. On the other side of the table, Mrs. Miner seemed to be trying to make herself small.

Before I had finished talking, Johnson turned on her. He shouted in a terrible, broken voice: "What are you trying to do? Get Jamie killed? Is that what you're trying to do?"

Her brown eyes rolled in apprehension. "I thought if I could find Fred."

"You thought! Nobody told you to think. I left strict orders that nobody was to go to the authorities." He was breathing fast. His face was swollen tight with blood and anger.

His wife laid a hand on his shoulder. "Abel, please. She meant well. Please don't excite yourself, darling."

"How can I help it? Why did you let her go?"

"I didn't know she'd left. Anyway, it's done no harm. Mr. Cross isn't the police. But he's half convinced me that we ought to call them."

"I agree, Abe," Seifel said from the doorway. "There's no sense in fooling around with a gang of kidnappers."

"I absolutely forbid it." Johnson took a few faltering steps and leaned on a corner of the table. "I'm not taking any chances with my boy's life. Anybody who thinks he's going to is going to have to do it over my dead body."

His wife regarded him anxiously. His mention of death was uncomfortably close to the literal truth. He looked very ill. She said, in the tone of a nurse humoring a patient:

"Don't upset yourself, dear. We'll do as you say. Nobody's going to call them."

Seifel came up beside me and spoke in my ear: "Ask him how long he intends to wait. This is serious."

"Why don't you?"

"He won't take suggestions from me. When I try to argue, he blows his top. It's a pretty mess, I'm telling you."

I said: "How long do you want us to wait, Mr. Johnson?" His wife gave me an appealing glance, and I added: "I think you're making a mistake, but I won't act until I have your go-ahead."

"You're damned right you won't." He lifted his sagging head. "They said in the letter they'd have him back today. I've done my part in the bargain. If there's any justice or any mercy, they'll do their part. We'll give them until midnight tonight." He threw a fierce look at Mrs. Miner: "You hear that?"

"Yessir, I hear it. I promise I'll stay right here. But what about Fred?"

"What about him?"

"He's gone, too."

"I know that, Mrs. Miner. If I thought that he was responsible for this, I—" Johnson choked on his emotion.

Mrs. Johnson took his arm and led him to the door. "Darling, you should lie down. You've had such a hard morning."

"I won't lie down. I couldn't possibly rest." But the heavy voice had faded into querulousness. He went along with her.

Seifel's bright satiric glance followed them out. "Brother, what a situation. Abe's carrying a coronary, you know. This stuff is murder. I practically had to lift him into the car at Sapphire Beach, when he got off the train."

He took a fresh white handkerchief from his breast-pocket, unfolded it, and wiped his forehead. He had a lot of forehead.

"Shouldn't he be seen by a doctor?"

"Helen will know what's best. She's an ex-nurse. As a matter of fact, she nursed Abe through his coronary. Helen's a very wonderful girl, in my opinion."

I disliked his proprietary tone. The wire Helen Johnson walked was higher and thinner than most people's, but she seemed to have somebody ready to catch her if she fell.

Mrs. Miner left the kitchen, carrying a silver coffee-service on a tray. Her red-rimmed eyes gazed straight ahead, fixed on some desolate scene in the distant regions of her mind.

Ann came around the table with the plate of sandwiches. She thrust it under Seifel's nose. "Have a sandwich, Mr. Seifel. You look hungry." Her furious blush had dwindled to oval patched on her cheekbones.

"Hi there, Annie. Thanks, I will." He took a sandwich and lifted the top to examine its contents. "Salmon I like. What are you doing in *cette galère?* Hired yourself out as a cook? I hear there's money in it."

"Mrs. Miner made the sandwiches," she answered primly. "I'm Mr. Cross's assistant, or had you forgotten? I understand your memory is abominable."

He patted her shoulder, simultaneously taking a bite of his sandwich. "At least the salmon is good," he said in a sandwich-thickened voice. "What's the beef, Annie?"

Ann lost her poise completely. She thrust his hand away like a hurt adolescent: "Don't you call me Annie. I hate that name."

"Miss Devon, then. Did I do anything?" He made a deprecatory face, but he seemed to be enjoying the situation.

"You know what you did. Your memory's not that bad. It's not as bad as your morals."

"Hey, wait a minute."

"I won't. You lied to me last night. You said you had a client from out of town. You stood me up so you could entertain Mrs. Johnson."

"Mrs. Johnson *and* Mr. Johnson. They're clients; aren't they? And they're from out of town. This is outside the city limits, isn't it?"

"Go on," she said. "*Talk* like a lawyer. You won't change the fact that you lied. I hate lawyers." A single tear ran down her cheek and dropped from the point of her chin into the plate of sandwiches she was holding.

I reached across Seifel and took one. "If you two want to finish this off in private, I'll go and sit in the car."

Seifel turned on a smile. "Sorry, old man. Don't mind us. Miss Devon and I are old sparring-partners."

"There are better times and places."

Ann left the room with a backward look at Seifel which was meant to be withering and was only pathetic. She seemed to have fallen hard, and nobody had caught her. My dislike of Seifel was turning acute.

"Women!" he said, with a humorous lift of his shoulders.

"Ann Devon's my favorite young woman."

"Mine, too. In my book she's the complete darling. But even the best of them let their emotions get out of kilter now and then. They can never understand that business is business. They want to make everything into a personal issue."

"A lot of things are."

"Come on now," he said heartily, "let's have a little masculine solidarity here."

I didn't smile.

He changed his manner with an actorish facility and became the earnest young lawyer: "What do you propose to do, Mr. Cross?"

"Wait."

"It's a long time till midnight. Can we afford to wait? Can the boy afford it?"

"We have to. Johnson could easily die of chagrin if we don't. In any case, it won't affect the boy's chances much. If they intended to kill him, he's dead now."

"You're not serious?"

"I'm afraid I am. He's a keen, observant boy. Jamie knows who snatched him, if he's alive. He'd make a good witness, and they must be aware of that."

His face registered horror, but Seifel was watching me

coolly from some internal center of self-love: "I hope to heaven Fred Miner isn't in it. I defended him, you know, on the manslaughter charge. Johnson asked me to do it."

"I share the hope. I guess we all do. Incidentally, I'd like to get the complete dope on that charge. There's no doubt he was guilty?"

"None at all. He never denied it."

"And you're absolutely sure it was an accident?"

He regarded me quizzically. "I'm never absolutely sure of anything. Beyond a reasonable doubt is the test we lawyers use. I have no reasonable doubt about it."

"Have they identified the victim yet?"

"Not so far as I know. I haven't been in touch with Dressen lately." Sam Dressen was the sheriff's indentification officer. "Anyway, he's a bit of a weak-willie in his job, if you want my opinion. Washington sent back the prints he took of the corpse. Apparently they were too smeared and faint for classification. By the time they shot them back, the body was buried. Last time I talked to Dressen, he was trying to trace the man through the cleaner's marks on the suit he was wearing. He promised to let me know if anything came of it."

"But nothing has."

"I guess not. For all we know, the fellow dropped from the sky. Which was fine for our case, of course. Fred wouldn't have got off so easy if the man he killed had had friends and relatives bringing pressure."

"It's a strange thing nobody claimed the body," I said. "Wasn't there any identification on it at all? No wallet? No driver's license?"

"Nothing like that. You'd think the guy deliberately wiped out his own identity."

"Did you see him?"

"Yes, I took a look at him in the morgue." Seifel's gaze turned inward. "I've seen prettier sights. There wasn't much left of his face. The fog-lamp smashed right into it as he fell. The pathologist said he died instantly. It was rather a shaking experience, I can tell you. I don't do much work in that line, you know. Seems he was a young fellow, about my age." His eyes sharpened again: "You don't suppose there's some connection between that accident and this?"

"Miner's in both. The things a man does are always connected in some way."

He raised his palm: "Let's not get into philosophy. Afraid I have to shove off now, old man. I have a luncheon engagement and I'm half an hour late already. I'll be in my office this afternoon."

"I'll probably drop by."

"Do that."

He started out, but I detained him. "Johnson left the fifty thousand at the station newsstand?"

"Of course. I was with him. That is, I stayed in my car."

"How did he happen to have so much money on hand?"

"Abe keeps a large savings account. He still likes to take an occasional flyer in real estate. Now I really must run."

He waved his hand and trotted out, the pads on his shoulders flopping like clumsy wings. I went through the butler's pantry, which was stocked as a bar, into the dining-room. The white refectory table was set for breakfast. Ham and eggs and toast lay cold and untouched on the plates. It was as if three breakfasters had been annihilated by a natural cataclysm as they sat down to eat.

Through the French windows that opened on the patio, a changing green light was thrown by the pool. I heard a murmur of voices and followed it outside. Ann and Mrs. Johnson were sitting in the green shade of an umbrella table at the end of the pool, conversing quietly over coffee cups.

Ann looked up and saw that I was alone. Her face showed mingled relief and disappointment. But it was Helen Johnson who said, in some surprise: "Is Larry gone?"

"He mentioned a luncheon engagement."

She frowned into her cup. "I do wish he'd stayed." She added with an almost embarrassing candor: "One needs a man around at a time alike this. Abel's pretty much of a broken reed. Not that I blame him. It's not his fault, dear man." She remembered her manners suddenly. "Sit down, Mr. Cross. Let me pour you some coffee."

"Thank you." I sat between them on a fishnet chair. "Is your husband all right?"

"I think so. I persuaded him to take a sedative and get some rest. Mrs. Miner is making up his bed. If he survived the first awful shock of that ransom letter—he'll survive anything. Still, I hate to be left alone with him."

"Won't Mrs. Miner be within reach?"

"Oh, yes. She's a good soul. Unfortunately, Amy Miner depresses me. She's what my husband calls a bleeding heart, I'm afraid. I'm talking like one myself." She drew a hand slowly across her eyes. "I'm talking much too much. It's the reaction. I oughtn't to have stayed alone here this morning. We thought there might be a phone call from them, you see. I waited for one, and the waiting just about drove me crazy. The morning lasted for years. I could actually feel my hair turning gray. It hasn't though, has it?" She ran white fingers through her hair. "Somebody shut me up, please."

Ann said impulsively: "I'll stay with you if you like."

"I would like, very much." Helen Johnson reached for her hand across the table. "it's sweet of you to offer. You're sure I'm not interfering with your plans?"

Ann looked at me with a Mona Lisa smile. "Howie, you don't mind if I stay with Helen?"

It seemed to me that dealing with women was like playing blindfold chess against unidentified opponents. Ann had never hinted that she was in love with Larry Seifel, or even that she knew him. I had had a vain suspicion now and then that she was secretly rather fond of me. Now a shadowy triangle was taking shape between her and Seifel and Helen Johnson. I didn't like it, but I said:

"Why should I? I have things to do. I won't be needing you. You're more use here."

"What things, Mr. Cross?" Helen Johnson's tone was

sharp. Under other circumstances I would have resented it.

"For one thing, I'm going into Fred Miner's background. How long have you known him, Mrs. Johnson?"

"Quite a long time, since 1945. He was in the Navy Hospital in San Diego. I was in charge of the orthopedic wards."

"Before your marriage?"

"Naturally. I was a lieutenant in the nursing corps."

"Fred was a friend of yours, then, as well as an employee."

"I gave him his job, if that's what you mean. Abel isn't allowed to drive, and I dislike driving. Fred needed light work: he's on partial disability. He was pleasant to have around. I suppose I was mainly responsible for keeping him on after that dreadful affair in February. I thought he should be given another chance."

"Why?"

She glanced at me sharply. "Didn't you?"

"I did. But I'm interested in your reason."

"Why, I—" She stammered and paused. "I believe in tolerance, I suppose. I've had bad breaks in my own life, and people have been tolerant with me. I try to pass it on."

"You're a generous woman."

"I wouldn't say that. At the moment I'm quite confused. In a thing like this, it's hard to keep hold of reality. When I let myself go I'm suspicious of everyone."

The conversation was obviously becoming a strain on her. Ann shook her head and frowned slightly.

I finished my black coffee and stood up. "Is it all right with you if I make a few inquiries in town? We should see whether the money's been picked up; there may have been a witness. I think you can trust my discretion."

"Do as you think best, Mr. Cross." Her gaze was dark and deep, lit by shifting green lights. "I have to trust someone, don't I?"

Going back along the curved side of the pool, I kept away

from the water's edge. I had a strange fear of falling in, though I had never been afraid of water.

CHAPTER
6

There was a witness, but he was blind. A small gray sign on the newsstand counter said: BLIND OPERATOR. The man behind the counter wore frosted glasses and spoke in the slow, clear accents of the sightless:

"What can I do for you, sir?"

I had just stepped into the shop, and hadn't spoken. "How did you know I was a man?" I knew by experience that sightless people seldom resented a direct reference to their loss.

He smiled. "Your footsteps, naturally. I'm sensitive to sound. You're a fairly big man, I'd guess. About six feet?"

"You hit it on the nose."

"I usually do. I'm five foot nine myself, you're about three inches taller. It's not too hard to estimate the level of the mouth. Now your weight. About one sixty-five?"

"One eighty," I said, "unfortunately."

"You're light on your feet for one eighty. Just a second, now. I'll guess your age."

"Aren't you getting into the psychic department?"

"No, sir. Voices change with the years, just like faces do. I'd say you're thirty-five, give or take a couple."

"Close enough. I'm thirty-seven."

"I'm practically never more than two years out. Bet a quarter you can't guess my age, though."

"Taken." I looked at the unlined brow, the carefully brushed black hair, the serene smiling mouth. "About thirty?"

"Forty-one!" he announced with gusto. "I lead a quiet life." He pushed a jar with a slotted lid across the counter. It was half full of quarters. "Drop your two bits in here. It goes to the Braille fund." He nodded briskly when he heard the fall of the coin. "Now what can I do for *you?*"

"Someone left a suitcase outside here this morning. Behind your newspaper rack."

He thought for a moment. "About eleven o'clock?"

"Exactly."

"So that's what it was. I thought I saw a suitcase."

"I beg your pardon."

"That's just a manner of speaking," he explained. "I see with my ears and touch and sense of smell. You've just been out in the country, haven't you? I can smell country on you."

"Right again." I was beginning to hope that the kidnappers had outwitted themselves in choosing this blind man's store for their money-drop. He made a point of noticing everything. "About the suitcase, it was left there shortly before eleven."

"Did you leave it?"

"A friend of mine did."

"He shouldn't have left it out there. I'd have kept it behind the counter for him. Was it stolen?"

"I wouldn't say it was stolen. It's simply gone. I think it was gone a few minutes after eleven."

He raised his sightless forehead. "Your friend doesn't think I took it?"

"Certainly not. I'm trying to trace the suitcase. I thought perhaps you could help me."

"You're a policeman?"

"I'm County Probation Officer. Howard Cross."

"Joe Trentino." He held out his hand. "I'm glad to meet you, Mr. Cross, heard your talk on the radio last winter. The one on juvenile delinquency. Now let me think."

His hand, when I had shaken it, returned to the jar of coins and twirled it on the glass counter-top as he concentrated:

"The ten fifty-five was in. It was standing there when I heard that suitcase plop down on the platform. It wasn't a big one, was it? Then somebody walked away. Your friend a heavy, older man? I couldn't see him too well, there was too much interference from the train."

"You're a wonder, Joe."

"Quiet," he said. "I'm listening. I had a couple of customers from the train, they wanted *Racing Forms*. They didn't stop at the newspaper rack. I guess they already got their papers before they left L.A. Hold it a minute. I had another customer, right after the train pulled out. He brought in a paper from the rack, a *News*. Now which one was it?"

He tapped his forehead lightly with blunt fingers. I watched him with a sense of strangeness growing on me. His awareness of the life around him seemed almost supernatural.

His tongue clicked. "It was one of the bellhops from down the street, they come in here all the time. I can tell them by the way they walk, by the way they handle a coin. He flipped his dime on the counter. Now which one was it? I know it was one of the boys from Pacific Inn."

Water started from the pores of his face. It was an arduous job, reconstructing reality from blowing wisps of sound.

"By golly!" he said. "He was carrying the suitcase. He picked it up before he came in. I heard it bump on the door-frame. I think it was Sandy, the one they call Sandy. He usually passes the time of day, but he didn't say a word to me. I wondered why he didn't speak. Was he stealing it?"

"No, probably he was just doing his job. Somebody sent him for it. I can't tell you any more about it right now, Joe." I caught myself up short. I had almost said: you'll read it in the papers. "Thanks for your trouble."

"No trouble at all," he said, with the water running down his face. "Drop in any time, Mr. Cross."

The Pacific Inn was a low, rambling building with sweeping tropical eaves and a deep veranda screened with split bamboo. Diagonally across from the railway station and in full sight of the newsstand, its various wings and bungalows occupied half a city block. As buildings went in Southern California, the Inn was an antique. Oldtimers at the courthouse remembered when it had been an international water-resort, crowded in season with dubious European aristocrats and genuine movie stars. That was before the great earthquake of the twenties cracked its plaster, before the economic earthquake a few years later cut off its clientele.

Since then the prosperous center of town had shifted uphill, away from the harbor and the railroad tracks. The Inn hung on, sinking gradually from second-rate to disreputable. It became the scene of weekend parties from Long Beach and Los Angeles, haunt of race-track touts, brief resting-place for touring stock-companies and itinerant salesmen. My work had taken me to it more than once.

Its atmosphere of depression surrounded me as I climbed the steps. A couple of old men, permanent residents of the bungalows, were propped on cane chairs against the wall like living souvenirs of the past. Their tortoise gaze followed me across the veranda. The lobby inside was dark-beamed and dusty. It hadn't changed in ten years. From one wall a grizzly's head snarled through the murk at an elk's head on the opposite wall. There were no humans.

I rang the handbell at the abandoned desk. From the dark bowels of the building, a little man in a faded blue uniform came trotting. His tight round stomach poked out gnomishly under the tunic.

"Desk-clerk's gone to lunch. You want a room?" Under the pillbox hat, the hair was sparse and faded brown, the color of drought-killed grass.

"Your name Sandy?"

He looked me over, trying to place me, and I returned the look. I guessed that he was a jockey grown too heavy to ride. He had the bantam cockiness, the knowing eyes, the sharp, strained youthfulness that had never dared to let itself mature. Money would talk to him. Probably nothing else would.

"What's your business, mister? You got to talk to the manager if you're selling. He's not here."

"I'm looking for a friend of mine. He carries a small black suitcase."

Boredom glazed his eyes. "Lots of people carry small black suitcases. The woods is full of them."

"This particular one was left at the station newsstand this morning. You picked it up about eleven o'clock."

I picked it up? Not me." Leaning on the desk, he crossed his stubby legs and looked up at the ceiling.

"Joe Trentino recognized you."

"He's seeing better lately? Nuts."

I didn't have money to use on him. Fear would have to do. "Listen to me, Sandy. That suitcase was hot. The longer you won't talk, the deeper you're in."

"Who you kidding?" But his gaze came down from the ceiling, met mine, and sank below it. "You a cop?"

"Close enough. That suitcase contained evidence of a felony. Right now you're an accomplice after the fact."

I watched fear grow in him like a sudden chill pinching his mouth and nostrils. "I handle a lot of suitcases. How do I know what's in them? You can't pin nothing on me." His mouth stayed open, showing broken teeth.

"You're either an accomplice or a witness."

"You can't bum-rap me," his fear chattered.

"Nobody's trying to, Sandy. I don't want your blood. I want your information. Is my friend staying here?"

"No," he said. "No, sir. You mean that one that sent me for the black suitcase?"

"That's the one. Did he pay you to keep quiet about it?"

"No, sir. He overtipped me, that's all. I figured there was something out of line. I don't mean il*l*egal, nothing like a felony. It's just most of the customers nowadays you got to use a chisel to peel a nickel off their palms. He slipped me two bucks for walking across the street."

"Tell me about him."

"I thought he was going to register when he came in, that

he was just off the train. No luggage, though. He told me he left his suitcase at the station, told me where it was.'' He held out his hands, palms upward. ''What should I do, tell him I was too ritzy to tote a bag? Could I know it was hot?''

''He also told you not to speak to Joe at the newsstand. Didn't he?''

Sandy looked everywhere but at me. The dismal surroundings seemed to sadden him. ''I don't remember. If he did, I must have figured it was a gag of some kind. What did Joe say?''

''Just what he heard. You do the same. Except that you have eyes.''

''You want a description?''

''As full a one as you can give me.''

''Is this going into court? I wouldn't make a good witness in court. I'm nervous.''

''Quit stalling, boy. You're one step away from being booked yourself. He paid you more than two dollars, and you knew very well it wasn't legit.''

''Honest to God, cross my heart.'' His fingers crossed and recrossed his faded blue breast. ''Two bucks was all it was. Would I risk a felony rap for a lousy two bucks? Do I look gone in the upper story?''

''I won't answer that one, Sandy. You are if you won't talk.''

''I'll talk, don't worry. But you can't make me say I knew. I didn't. I still don't. What was it, stolen goods? Marijuana?''

''You're wasting time. Let's have a complete description.''

He took a deep breath. It wheezed in his throat and swelled his chest out like a pouter pigeon's. ''Okay, I said I'd cooperate, that's my policy. Let's see, he was about your size, maybe a little shorter. Definitely fatter. A pretty ugly puss, if you ask me, I should of known he was a hustler. Whisky eyes—you know what I mean?—a sort of pinky blue color. He was pretty well dressed, though, a sharp dresser. Brown slacks and light tan jacket, yellow sport shirt. I like good clothes myself. I notice clothes. He had these two-tone shoes, brown and doeskin or whatever they call it. Real sharp.''

"A young man?"

"Naw, I wouldn't call him young. Middle-aged is more like it, maybe in his fifties. One thing I noticed about him. He had a hat on—brown snap-brim—but under it I think he was wearing a toupee. You know how they look at the back, sort of funny around the edges, like they didn't belong to the neck?"

"You have eyes all right. What color?"

"Brown, sort of a dark reddish brown."

"Over-all impression?"

"I tabbed him strictly from hunger, but putting on a front. You follow me? We see a lot of them: actors and pitchmen out of a job, ex-bookies peddling tips from the horse's brother—that sort of stuff, with barely one nickel to rub against another, but keeping the old front up. When he slipped me folding money, you could have knocked me over with a bulldozer."

"Did he pay you before or after?"

"One buck when he sent me, the other when I came back. He was waiting on the veranda when I came back. What was in that suitcase? It didn't feel heavy to me."

"I'll tell you when I find out. Where did he go with it?"

"He marched off down the street. I thought he was going to register—"

"You said that. Which way?"

"Across the railroad tracks."

"Come out and show me."

He followed me to the veranda steps, and pointed west towards the harbor:

"I didn't wait to see where he went. He just started walking that way. He walked as if his feet hurt him."

"Carrying the suitcase?"

"Yeah, sure. But now you mention it, he had a topcoat with him. He carried the suitcase under his arm, with the topcoat kind of slung over it."

"Did he cross the street?"

"Not that I saw. He didn't go back to the station, anyway."
I thanked him and went west.

CHAPTER
7

The bellhop's story, true or false, had touched an internal
valve that charged my blood with adrenalin. I walked
quickly across the railroad tracks, with no definite idea of
where I was going. All I had was a good description and a
couple of fairly rickety assumptions.

One was that the quarry wouldn't have gone far on the
open street with a black suitcase under his arm. If he had
stepped into a waiting car and left town immediately, there
wasn't much I could do by myself. As if to emphasize the
point, a cruising patrol car passed me slowly. A plainclothesman I didn't recognize lifted his hand to the window.

The anomaly of my position, halfway between the policeman and civilian, hit me hard. I felt a powerful impulse to
break my word to Johnson, stop the car, set off an all-points
alarm. The moment passed. The prowl car drove out of
hearing, dragging the impulse with it. I had to act within the
limits Johnson had imposed, or not act at all.

It was nearly two by my watch, almost three hours since
the double play with the suitcase. But there was a chance
that my man was still in town. Though I assumed as a
matter of course that he came from out of town, he had
probably spent the night here, since the ransom letter had
been mailed the day before. If he had, he had probably
stayed fairly close to the station. And there was a chance in

a hundred, perhaps one in fifty, that he was holed up in one of the waterfront hotels, waiting for night.

The harbor area had once been advertised as the Juan-les-Pins of the West. The treacherous years and an unwise city council had given it over to penny arcades and salt-water-taffy booths, carrousels, open-front beer-joints, a grab-bag assortment of hostelries. The latter ranged from fishermen's flops to fairly respectable motels. I had been in all of them at one time or another.

A Spanish-American chambermaid in the Delmar Motel, who believed her virtue to be under constant attack, had thrown ammonia in a guest's face. Three years' probation with psychiatric treatment. A seventeen-year-old boy, a junior in high school, who was on probation for grand theft automobile, rented a room in the Gloria in order to commit suicide. It took us eighteen hours to bring him out of barbiturate coma. Now he was due to be graduated from college in a month.

I shook the memories off and looked outward. Girls and children in swimsuits, T-shirted men and boys, were strolling along the sea-wall and on the wharf. The white sand below the sea-wall was strewn with brightly costumed bathers. From the edge of the beach, a crew of oarsmen was launching a cedar shell. It slid out onto the water and began to walk on its oars like a waterbug, with eight crewcut heads nodding in unison.

I stepped into the narrow bamboo-furnished lobby of the Gloria Hotel. The desk clerk remembered me. He was a thin, ageless Italian who had always been there. I described my man. No, he hadn't seen anyone of that description, today or yesterday. Sorry we can't help you, Mr. Cross.

At the Delmar, the ammonia-tossing chambermaid had married the manager and risen to key-girl. Her large black eyes grew larger when I entered. She still had a year to go.

"Mr. Cross? You want to see me?"

"Relax, Secundina. Miss Devon tells me you're doing fine."

She came out through the swinging door beside the

registration counter, a beautiful girl in a Spanish blouse, with ribbons in her hair. The management liked atmosphere.

"Miss Devon is a good woman," she stated. "I am not afraid no more—any more." She swung her arms in a free movement in order to demonstrate that she was not afraid. The ribbons fluttered.

I said: "I'm looking for a man."

"What man? He is staying here?"

"You tell me, Secundina." I described him.

"He is not one of our guests," she said with certainty. "*Un momento*. Wait a minute. I theenk—I think I have seen him."

"When was this?"

"This morning. I was sweeping the veranda. The sand blows from the beach." Her hand moved laterally, imitating the sand. "This big old man went by in the street, walking very queeckly."

She began to walk, very queeckly, in a small circle of which I was the hub. Her expert mimicry included a sore-footed limp. It ended with a dancer's heel-and-toe.

"Can you remember what time this morning?"

Her carmine mouth was weighted with thought. "Eleven o'clock? Five minutes after? Ten minutes? It was soon after eleven. I opened the office at eleven."

"Did you notice, was he carrying anything?"

She considered the question, her finger twiddling a lower lip. "I am not sure. Perhaps a coat? I hardly looked at him."

"You didn't see where he went?"

"That way, in the direction of the Harbormaster's office." She pointed northward, parallel with the shoreline.

"And he was hurrying?"

"Ah, yes, very queeckly!"

She began to demonstrate the limping hustle again. I raised my hand in a traffic officer's gesture. She smiled and desisted. I touched the lifted hand to the brim of my hat and started out. She called after me:

"Say hello to Miss Devon!"

The lift I had got from Secundina, the lift I always got

when fear took a setback, faded rapidly on the pavement. There was nothing in the direction she had indicated but a dollar doss over a fried-fish place. FRIED FISH. ROOMS ONE DOLLAR. TRY OUR SMOKED FISH SPECIAL. JUMBO SHRIMP. The greasy counterman who doubled as roomclerk had never seen my man. His close mouth wouldn't have opened if he had.

The harbormaster's Quonset and jetty lay in the corner of the cove where the Point curved out from the shore. The blank-walled bath-house in front of it was loud as a monkeyhouse with teen-age whistles and hoots and ululations. Beyond it, across the base of the landspit, deep-sea breakers pounded a steep shore. The desolate beach, eaten at the edge by dangerous currents, was closed to swimmers. It pullulated with gulls. They rose like an inverted snowstorm, and veered seaward.

The asphalt road across the base of the point was sandblown and salt-pitted and led nowhere. The dancing pavilion it had served had been smashed by a winter storm some years ago. Nothing remained of the pavilion but crumbling concrete bulkheads and a large, weathered billboard: DINE AND DANCE TO THE MUSIC OF THE WAVES.

A few cars were parked along the edge of the road, nosed into the sand-drifts on its seaward side. There were a couple of empty jalopies, a family eating picnic-lunch in their station wagon, an old truck piled with black and brown fishing-nets. A black and brown mongrel with a Doberman head barked violently from the rear of the truck as I passed, wagging his tail in self-congratulation.

"Be a hero," I told him. His bark made the whole truck shake. The gulls coming in from the sea flew out again, blown between blue layers of sea and sky.

Another car was parked near the truck, almost hidden behind the Dine and Dance billboard. The tracks it had made in the sand were blowing over but still visible. It was a prewar Chrysler sedan, painted blue, with a Los Angeles license number. I looked in through the open rear window. A new black suitcase lay open on the back seat, empty.

A man reclined on the front seat half covered by a brown topcoat. His head was jammed into the corner between the right-hand door and the back of the seat, his legs twisted under the steering wheel. When I opened the door a brown toupe detached itself from his skull and draped itself across the toe of my shoe. From the side of his neck the red plastic handle of an icepick stood out like a terrible carbuncle.

The registration card had been ripped from its holder on the steering-post. The car keys hung from the ignition, but no identification was attached to them. I went through the pockets of the dead man's mohair jacket and chocolate gabardine slacks. They contained a pocket comb in a leatherette case marked with the initials A.G.L., a handkerchief, an unopened packet of chlorophyll gum, and the yellow stub of a theater ticket. Nothing else.

Sand flies were gathered on the dead face. I covered it with the topcoat and closed the door gently. When I went back past the truck, the dog was still barking and wagging. The picnickers in the station wagon were laughing over Coke bottles. I turned away from them. Above the sea the gulls were wheeling, wings glinting in the sun, turning like slow electrons in blue eternity.

I phoned Helen Johnson from the Harbormaster's office and told her why I had to call the police.

CHAPTER
8

I met her an hour later in what passed for the local morgue. It was actually the back room of an undertaking establishment near the courthouse. The dead man had been brought there to wait for the deputy coroner, who had gone sailing. Cause of death was not in doubt, but there would have to be an autopsy.

Identity was in doubt. The Highway Patrol had given us rapid service on the license number, and were tracing the car itself. It had been licensed in Los Angeles to one Kerry Smith, who gave his address as the Sunset Hotel, a transients' hostel near Union Station. The Sunset Hotel reported that no Kerry Smith had been registered there, at least since the first of the year; and the name Kerry Smith did not agree with the initials A.G.L.

The anonymous man lay on a rubber-tired table against a coldly sweating concrete wall. Sandy the bellhop had looked down at his face, nodded in nervous recognition, and been booked as a material witness. A few minutes after Sandy was led away protesting, Helen Johnson came in out of the sunlight. She was dressed in high fashion, in hat and veil and gloves. The color of the suit she had chosen was black. In the fluorescent light her hair looked almost black, and her eyes black. Ann Devon was with her.

Death, which banishes the dead to unimaginable distances, brings the living closer together sometimes. The two women linked arms and formed a unit against the silent wind blowing from those distances. Behind them Cleat, lieutenant of detectives, gnawed impatiently on a remnant of cigar. Our eight eyes were drawn to the body against the wall, and wavered away from it.

"What does it mean, Howie?" Ann said. Still in her working dress and flat-heeled shoes, she was shorter and shabbier than the other woman, like a younger sister or a poor relation.

"I don't know what it means. These are the facts. This man picked up the money at the station—the bellboy he sent for it identified both him and the suitcase. Then he walked the three blocks from the station to the beach, where he'd parked his car. Someone was waiting at the car, or followed him there, stabbed him with an icepick, and made off with the money. We don't know whether that someone was an accomplice in the kidnapping or not. We have no lead on who it was. Lieutenant Cleat's men are canvassing the waterfront now, trying to turn up a witness.''

Mrs. Johnson reached out as if to grasp me, but her black-gloved hand stayed empty in the air. "There's no sign of Jamie?''

"None. That doesn't mean anything. We didn't expect to find him here in town. This man was obviously detailed to collect the money. He couldn't have handled both the money and the boy. There must be at least one other—''

"Fred Miner?''

"That's our working hypothesis, ma'am,'' Cleat said heavily. "Miner's melted into thin air, along with the boy. It didn't happen by accident.''

"No.'' Her face began to crumple, then straightened itself. "I've been thinking wishfully. I hated to believe it.''

Cleat caught my eye and held it, rather grimly: "It's what I always say. Once a man starts to go bad, he's bound to go all the way.''

It was no time to argue. I said to Mrs. Johnson: "What does your husband think of this development?''

"I haven't dared tell him. I left him sleeping, poor dear. Well.'' She squared her shoulders and turned to Cleat. "You brought me her to see him, didn't you? I might as well get it over with.''

"We looked at it like this,'' Cleat said. "If him and Miner were in cahoots, you might have seen him with Miner some time, or maybe loitering around casing the joint. He certainly had a line on your routine, mail deliveries and such. I realize it's a painful ordeal, ma'am.''

"Not at all. I've frequently handled cadavers.''

Cleat's eyebrows jumped.

I said: "Mrs. Johnson was a nurse. But wouldn't Mrs. Miner be more likely—?''

"I got her waiting outside. Now, Mrs. Johnson, if you don't mind."

She and Ann approached the table. Cleat switched on a hanging lamp above it and adjusted the toupee. A.G.L. looked straight up into the light without blinking.

"I've never seen him."

Cleat removed the toupee. The bald head gleamed. Ann caught her breath and leaned forward, craning her neck sideways.

."Head's sunburnt on top," Cleat said. "I figure he didn't always wear the hairpiece."

"No," Helen Johnson said clearly. "I have never seen him."

Ann· said nothing. They went out together. Ann called back through the closing door. "I'll be in the office."

The door was opened again almost immediately, and Mrs. Miner came in. Cleat seized her roughly by the arm:

"I want you to take a good hard look now, Mrs. what's your first name?"

"Amy."

"I want the truth now, Amy. You know him, say so. You have any doubts, I'll give you a little while to make up your mind. That clear?"

"Yessir," she answered tonelessly.

"Whatever you do, don't lie to me, Amy. That's what they call suppressing evidence. It's just as bad as the original crime itself. That clear?"

"Yessir."

"You know and I know," Cleat said, "that if this fella here was mixed up with your husband, you'd know it. You couldn't help knowing it—"

"Hire a hall, Lieutenant," I said.

Amy Miner looked at me gratefully. She, too, had changed to different clothes, a knitted jersey suit that sagged on her thin body. I guessed that she had inherited it from Mrs. Johnson, or from a plumper version of herself.

Cleat placed an arm around her back and propelled her to the table. She winced away, more from Cleat than from the body. Cleat jerked her back by the arm. He hated criminals. He hated anyone connected with criminals.

I moved up behind him. "Easy, Lieutenant."

His voice remained perfectly bland. "Now watch it, Amy." With a showman's gesture, he manipulated the toupee.

Her breath made a small shrill sighing in her nose. "No, I never saw him."

"Wait now, just take your time." He whisked the toupee off.

"No," she said. "I never saw him, with Fred or anybody else."

"His initials are A.G.L. Doesn't that suggest a name to you?"

"No. Can I go now?"

"Take one more good look."

She looked down and wagged her head sharply, twice. "No. And I can tell you, my Fred didn't do it. He never lifted his hand against man or beast. Never in all the years I've know him."

"What about last February?" Cleat said.

"That was an accident."

"Maybe. This was no accident. Maybe that wasn't either. We got two unidentified bodies now. They're piling up like cordwood. Where's Fred, Amy?"

She said in a still, cold fury: "If I knew I wouldn't tell you."

"Do you know?" Cleat towered over her, working his eyebrows.

"I said I didn't. Ask me some more if you want, though."

Balling his fist, Cleat thrust it up into contact with her chin, and held it there. They stared into each other's eyes like trysting lovers. Cleat moved his fist upward slightly. Her head snapped back.

She stepped away. Her features sharpened to a cutting edge. "Rough me up, why don't you? Fred isn't here to protect me."

"Where is he then? You're his wife. He wouldn't leave without telling you."

"He said he was coming into town, to see Mr. Linebarge. That's all he said."

Cleat glanced questioningly at me.

"She's telling the truth," I said. "Miner came to my office this morning. I told you that."

Cleat turned back to the woman, hunching his shoulders melodramatically. "What else did he tell you, Amy?"

"Nothing."

"Who's A.G.L. here?"

"I don't know," she said.

He lifted his open hand, which resembled a rough-cut piece of one-inch planking. Her eyes followed its movement in fascination.

I stepped between them facing Cleat. "Break it up, Lieutenant. If you want to question her, use words. You have a few."

There was a brisk tapping on the door.

"I'm doing my job," he said. "It wouldn't be so tough if you'd do yours. I don't care how you treat your Goddamn clients. Only keep them in line, that's all I ask. Keep them out of trouble, out of my hair."

I had no good answer. Miner had made me vulnerable.

The door swung wide, flooding half of the room with sunlight. The uniformed policeman on guard outside said, with the air of a butler announcing a V.I.P.: "Mr. Forest is here, from the F.B.I."

"Fine." Cleat swung his cigar toward Amy Miner: "I want this biddy locked up as a material witness. No bail."

"Witness to what?" she cried on a rising note. "You can't put me in jail. I haven't done anything."

"It's for your own protection, Mrs. Miner." The formula came out pat. "We let you run around loose, you could end up in an alley with an icepick in *your* neck."

She turned to me, her thin torso leaning tensely forward from her hips: "How can he, Mr. Cross? I'm innocent. They haven't got nothing on Fred even."

"Lieutenant Cleat has the right," I said. "Your husband's under suspicion. They'll let you go as soon as he's cleared.''

''If,'' Cleat said.

She batted her eyes like a scared filly, and ran for the door and the sunlight. The man who was coming in caught her around the waist, immobilized her flailing arms and passed her to the police guard. The guard pushed her towards the black car that was waiting in the drive. Her angular shadow merged with the shadow of the car.

The young man in the doorway was florid and stocky. His silhouette was almost square in a double-breasted business suit.

''I'm Forest, Special Agent,'' he said briskly, and shook hands with efficient heartiness. ''Our technicians are coming down in the mobile unit, should be here very soon. I understand there's a ransom note?''

I quoted it, almost verbatim. It kept repeating itself in the back of my mind, like a song that was too ugly to forget.

Forest's quick brown eyes steadied and sobered. ''Nasty piece of work, eh? Who's in charge of the case here?''

''Lieutenant Cleat is. The *corpus* was found in the city. But the boy lives in the county. If Miner snatched him, the crime originated in the sheriff's territory.''

''You with the sheriff's department?''

''I'm a probation officer.'' I explained who Miner was, and my connection with the case.

Forest turned to Cleat. ''Call the sheriff, will you please, Lieutenant?'' He added in a rather doctrinaire tone: ''Cooperation with local agencies is our first principle.''

Cleat glanced involuntarily at the body on the table. It had been all his until now. ''Okay.'' He removed his cigar, threw it on the concrete floor, ground it to shreds with his heel, and left the room. A bleat of organ music came through the inner door before he closed it.

Forest went to the body. His practiced hands dove in and out of pockets. ''Ugly customer, eh?''

''Handsome is as handsome does. I searched him when I found him. Nothing useful, except a pocket comb with his initials, A.G.L. The murderer didn't want him identified too soon."

"He was stabbed, wasn't he? Where's the weapon?"

"It was done with an icepick. They're testing it for prints now. I don't think they're going to find any."

"Icepicked, eh? And hijacked. It could be a big-time mob at work. Fifty thousand is a lot of hay. The parents wealthy?"

"The father has half a million or so, according to the rumors."

"Like to talk to him."

"He's at home, ill. The mother's probably in my office now. It isn't far."

"She have the ransom letter?"

"I think she left it at home."

"We want to get to work on that. They're bringing our file along for comparison. *Modus operandi* is primary in a kidnap case. It's like a compulsion neurosis repeating itself. Not that it often gets a chance to repeat."

He shot his cuff with a peculiarly mechanical movement, and looked at his watch. I half expected him to suggest we synchronize our watches.

"Twenty past three," he said. "Let's get going. You can give me a rundown on the way and I'll check back here later."

We cut across the courthouse grounds. A trusty was mowing the lawn with a power mower. The cut grass smelled fresh and sweet, and after the pavement the springy turf was pleasant underfoot.

I talked and Forest listened. He listened well. I had the impression that my words were being recorded on rolls of permanent tape whizzing round in his skull.

CHAPTER
9

When we reached the County Annex, Ann was locking the door to the office. I introduced her to Fred.

"Has Mrs. Johnson gone home?"

"Yes," she said. "I promised to drive out after her. Helen shouldn't be alone, and she doesn't seem to have any friends or relatives available."

"You're a dutiful girl."

She flinched at the compliment, and bit her lower lip. "I have nothing better to do."

"I wonder, might I hitch a ride with you, Miss Devon?" Forest spoke very politely. Ann was pretty. "I'm not familiar with the local topography."

"Of course." She turned to me in a sudden flurry of impulse. "Howie, I have to talk to you, privately."

"Right now?"

"Please, if you have the time."

Forest put in swiftly: "That's all right. I'd like to look over your probation report on Miner."

Ann brought it out of the files and followed me into my office, closing the door. She stood with her hands behind her, looking down at the worn cork floor-covering between us:

"I'm afraid you're going to think a good deal less of me, after today."

"That little business with Seifel? Not a bit of it. It's even a hopeful sign. I was beginning to be afraid that all your feelings were for other people.''

"I'm really a jealous vixen under the skin. That's not what I wanted to say, though.''

"Strangely enough, I didn't think it was.''

"I'm in love with him,'' she said.

"I didn't even know that you and Seifel were friends.''

"We're not, exactly. I don't approve of him. He doesn't take me seriously at all. He baits me for being a blue-stocking. But ever since he came to the office that day—''

"What day?''

"It was in February, when he was working up the Miner case. He came in to ask some questions. You were up in the north end of the county, Alex was out. We got to talking, and he asked me to have lunch with him. I've been seeing him ever since.''

"It's no crime. Why the secrecy?''

"He doesn't want his mother to know. As a matter of fact, I didn't want you to know.''

"Both of your reasons sound peculiar to me.''

"Do they? I guess I'm a little ashamed of myself, Howie. He's not my type. Sometimes I think I hate him. All he's interested in is money and social success. He's a money-hungry egotist. How could I fall in love with a man like that? Yet I can't get him out of my head. I dream about him at night. What's happened to me, Howie?''

"First love, maybe. You're having a late adolescence. Better late than never.''

"You're laughing at me.''

"Is that so terrible? I admit I'm surprised, but I'm not exactly shocked. It's time he got married, anyway, and you, too.''

"You don't think he'd marry *me*? No. He'll wait for Mr. Johnson to die, and marry *her*.'' Her voice had sunk to a melodramatic whisper.

"You're making him out worse than he is. There's nothing the matter with Seifel a good woman couldn't fix.

He's simply spoiled. I'll bet a nickel his mother has spoiled him all his life.''

"She has. I've seen them together. He's just like a big cat, purring when she strokes him. Oh, I despise that man!''

"Uh-huh," I said.

She turned away and wiped her brimming eyes. Her voice came muffled through Kleenex: "Howie, there's something else. I'm sorry. This wasn't what I meant to talk about at all. You sort of drew it out of me.''

"Call me Torquemada.''

"No, don't joke now. This is serious. It may be important. I ought to have told you right away. I couldn't make myself. I don't know what's becoming of me, morally—''

"Buck up," I said loudly and firmly. "You have something to tell me. I'm here.''

"I've seen the dead man before, Howie.''

"Where?''

"With Larry Seifel. I was afraid to tell you.''

"Go on. When was this, lately?''

"It was in February, the day Fred Miner was tried. I met Larry at the door of the courtroom—we were going to have lunch together. He and this man were in the empty courtroom, talking.''

"Are you sure?''

"I wouldn't have spoken if I weren't. I couldn't forget that face, those reddish eyes. And the bald head. He wasn't wearing a toupee that day.''

"What were they talking about?''

"I didn't listen. They came to the door together. Larry shook hands with him, and said something about getting in touch with him in Los Angeles if he ever needed his help.''

"If Larry ever needed his help?''

"Yes. What are you going to do about, it, Howie?''

"Get a positive identification from Seifel, naturally. If he's willing to make one.''

She took hold of my arm with both hands, looking up at my face through tears. "Please don't tell him I told you.''

"Are you so crazy about him?"

"It's terrible. I feel lonely all the time I'm not seeing him."

"Even if he's mixed up in this business?"

She pressed her face against my shoulder. "He is mixed up in it, I know he is. I realized it as soon as I saw that man in the back of the mortuary. It doesn't seem to change my feeling."

The fine tremor of her nerves passed through her hands to my arm. Her hair had disarrayed itself. I smoothed it with my free hand.

"You're my good right arm, Ann. I don't want you going to pieces."

"I'm not." She straightened up, refastening bobby pins, regrouping her forces.

"Go home and take a rest. Forget about Mrs. Johnson. She's made of strong stuff, and doing perfectly well."

"So am I." She managed a smile. "Don't worry about me. I'll put on my public look. Actually, I'm better off with somebody else to think about."

"Do you like her?"

"Of course I do. I think she's a marvelous woman." Ann had already put on her public look. "Don't you?"

Helen Johnson's face was suddenly in my mind. I realized that she was a beautiful woman. Her beauty wasn't dazzling. It was simply there, something definite and solid that had never entirely left my mind from the moment I met her.

"Don't you?" Ann repeated with her Mona Lisa smile.

I refused to answer on the grounds that my reply might tend to incriminate me. "Beat it now, Ann. Forest is waiting for you."

"If I'm your good right arm, you won't tell Larry, will you?"

"Not unless I have to. But he'll know."

"I can't help that, can I?"

CHAPTER
10

Forest was sitting in Ann's chair with the typed report in his hand. He turned it face down on the desk and stood up.

"This man's record is excellent, at least on the surface. You're sure it's complete? No missing years or anything like that?"

"Linebarge does a thorough job," I said. "He used to be a cop, and he has to convince himself every time."

"He's convinced me. If this is the full story, unretouched, I can't see Miner in the role of kidnapper. A man doesn't often build up a solid record for twenty or thirty years, then turn around and commit a major crime. Of course there are exceptions: embezzlement, passional murder. But kidnapping for profit takes preparation. It doesn't come naturally to a normal man. Well, Miss Devon? Are we ready?"

"Ready," she answered with her best public smile.

"One thing occurred to me," he said from the doorway. "This hit-and-run he pleaded guilty to—is there any possibility it wasn't an accident? Murder by automobile is getting pretty common in these parts. Who was the victim?"

"Not identified, so far as I know."

"The courthouse people call him Mr. Nobody," Ann put in.

"Two of them, eh? This case has its puzzling aspects, all right." Forest held the door for Ann and closed it sharply behind him.

I sat down in the chair he had been warming, and phoned

Larry Seifel's office. A secretarial voice told me with sweet impatience that he was busy.

"Tell him it's Howard Cross, and I'm also busy."

"Very well, Mr. Goss."

His voice sounded higher and thinner over the wire. "Who is it speaking, please?"

"Cross. I'm in my office. I want to see you right away."

"Can't you come over here? I'm swamped with work, drawing up one of these complicated trusts. I lost the whole morning, you know."

I cut him short: "I'll expect you in twenty minutes, or less. On the way—do you know Watkins's Mortuary?"

"It's a block up from the courthouse, isn't it?"

"Right. Cleat's got a corpse there, in the back room. I want you to look at it before you come here. Tell Cleat I sent you."

"A corpse? Somebody I know?"

"You should be able to answer that question when you see him." I hung up.

Turning the Miner report over, I began to glance through it idly, and then to read it in earnest. I hadn't seen it since Larry submitted it for my approval the week before the hearing, and there were going to be questions about Fred Miner.

I skipped through the "Family Background" section, which reminded me that Frederick Andrew Miner had been born on an Ohio farm in 1916. His mother died two years after his birth and her place in his life was taken by his elder sister, Ella. Their father was a strict man, a member of the Mennonite sect whose motto was: "The Devil finds things for idle hands to do." The boy's hands were seldom idle. He worked full time on the farm in the spring and summer. In the winter he attended country school, and later a Union High School, where he specialized in "practical mechanics."

According to the records of the High School [the report went on] *Miner was a serious, plodding student with a good citizenship standing and great mechanical aptitude. He was, however, forced to leave school without being graduated, at the age of sixteen, and take a full-time job in a local garage. This shift was necessitated to a great extent by economic pressures. For a period of several years, while he was still in his teens, the boy was the mainstay of the family, his garage work providing the only regular cash-income the Miner family had. This was supplemented to some extent by Miner's winnings as a stock-car racing-driver at various local meets and county fairs.*

When the Depression lifted somewhat, Miner was enabled to borrow enough money, with his father's backing, to open a small filling-station of his own. This prospered, and by 1940 when he enlisted in the armed services, Miner was the proprietor of a filling-station and an attached "service" garage.

His initial desire, Miner states, was to become a fighter pilot in the U.S. Navy. Being unable to meet the educational requirements, he elected instead to become a ground crewman in the Naval air service. After a period of boot training at Norfolk, Va., he served at various Naval air bases on the West Coast, and rose, through diligent work and regular study, to the rating of Aviation Motor Machinist's Mate, First Class. While stationed at the Naval Air Station, San Diego, Miner met and married Amy Wolfe, daughter of a small businessman in San Diego, on Sept. 18, 1942. Their marriage, although childless, has been marked by steady and devoted companionship.

In the summer of 1943, Miner was ordered to Bremerton, Wash., to join the crew of the Eureka Bay, *an escort carrier then in the final stages of construction. Mrs. Miner followed her husband to Bremerton, and remained near him during the training and shakedown period. It was during this period, she states, that Miner "took his first drink," and discovered that he was unable to "hold his liquor." This fact is confirmed by Dr. Levinson, who describes Miner in his attached report as "a potential alcoholic, that is, a man who is psychologically and/or physiologically abnormally susceptible to the intoxicant and depressant effects of alcohol."*

Miner's first drinking episode, he frankly admits, was responsible for the only black mark on his Naval record. Failing to return aboard ship at the assigned time after a weekend pass, he was reduced to the rating of Aviation Machinist's Mate, Second Class. Within a year, however, Miner had recovered his First Class rating, and before his Naval career ended, he achieved the rating of Chief Aviation Motor Machinist.

Miner's contribution to his country's defense, a factor to which the community attaches some weight when the kind and degree of a man's punishment for a crime is in the balance, is sufficiently attested to by the attached letters from Captain Angus Drew, C.O. of the Eureka Bay, 1944–1945; Commander Julius Heckendorf, Executive Officer; and Lieutenant Elmer Morton, First Lieutenant and Damage Control Officer. "His diligence and devotion to duty," Comdr. Heckendorf writes, "were remarkable even in a branch of the service where such qualities are a normal expectation. His work was an inspiration to the men under him, and a source of satisfaction to his superiors." During Miner's service aboard the Eureka Bay the vessel participated in the Iwo Jima, Luzon and Okinawa invasions.

Towards the conclusion of the Okinawa campaign, Miner's Naval career was terminated in what Lieutenant Morton calls "a burst of glory." The Eureka Bay was struck by a Japanese "suicide" plane, which tore a hole in the flight deck and plunged through to the hangar deck. In the confusion that followed, Miner assumed responsibility for fighting the ensuing fire on the hangar deck, and the crew that he rallied was successful in bringing the blaze under control. Unfortunately, a bomb exploded in the wreckage of the "Kamikaze," throwing Miner against a bulkhead and fracturing his skull and spine. Flown to Guam and ultimately to the Naval Hospital in San Diego, Miner spent the greater part of the next year in a hospital bed. He was released from the service on a fifty-per-cent-disability pension in March 1946.

Immediately upon his release, Miner was offered a position as chauffeur with Mr. Abel Johnson, at that time the head of a San Diego real estate firm. He has been employed by Mr. Johnson since that time and has, to quote his employer's own words, "served us loyally and efficiently." Mr. Johnson is willing, if the Court see fits to grant probation, to continue Miner in his present position and to assume reasonable responsibility for his future good behavior (See memo. #8). Dr. Levison is of opinion that: "Miner in particular, and the community in general, need have nothing to worry about if he will eschew alcoholic beverages in any and all forms. Apart from his potential alcoholism, a condition which is by no means rare among wounded war veterans in general and men who have lost their mothers at an early age in particular, Miner presents a sound psychological configuration."

Turning to the circumstances of the accident itself, we find certain mitigating circumstances. One is the fact that Miner admits his guilt, and is sincerely repentant. Another is the fact that he was "on holiday" when the accident occurred. While no excuse can be made for drunken driving as such, the fact is that Miner's employers were both absent at the time, winter vacationing at their desert establishment, so that Miner cannot be charged with "drinking on duty." There is the further fact that, while Miner was found to be legally intoxicated at the time of his arrest, his victim was also under the influence of alcohol. The victim's blood was found to have an alcoholic content of 157 mg., from which it is arguable that the victim may have been at least partly responsible for the accident. As for the second and perhaps more serious charge against Miner, that of leaving the scene of a fatal accident without reporting it to the proper authorities, Miner himself claims that he was totally unaware of the accident's occurrence. Supporting his assertion, difficult as it is to believe due to the damage to the automobile and the evidence of violent impact, is Dr. Levinson's opinion that "a person of Miner's susceptibility to alcohol, with over 200 mg. of it in his blood, might very conceivably have run over a man without knowing it."

Miner himself can only be described as a willing and hopeful prospect for probation. There are no other violations in his record, and he says with every appearance of sincerity: "I intend to observe all laws in future. My failure to observe the laws against drunken driving and leaving the scene of an accident are a source of intense remorse to me. All I can say is that liquor was my downfall." His wife, Amy Wolfe Miner, states: "If ever a man has learned from experience, Fred has learned. I am equally responsible with Fred for letting him buy that bottle. We are both resolved that there will be no more bottles, Fred is a teetotaler from here on in."

We conclude that with his wife's support and that of his employers, Frederick A. Miner should be in a good position to rehabilitate himself under the guidance of the Probation Department. Such guidance should include a total ban on the consumption of alcoholic beverages, strict adherence to all laws in both letter and spirit, especially traffic laws, regular interviews with the probation authority, a course of indoctrination at the Alcoholism Center, and such other conditions as the Court may see fit to incorporate in its order.

ALEX S. LINEBARGE
Deputy Probation Officer

I put the report back in its folder and replaced it in the "M" file. Thorough as it was, it failed to answer some of the questions rising in my mind. The question Forest had asked, for instance: Could the involuntary manslaughter have been voluntary homicide? Was there a connection between the first anonymous body and the second, between both and Fred? Most important of all, and most difficult: What sort of a man was Miner?

No human personality peeped out between the lines of Alex Linebarge's unimaginative prose. To Alex, souls were either black or white. He had decided once and for all that Miner was white, and omitted those touches of tattletale gray that would have given reality to his sketch. There was a sense in which Miner, in spite of the laborious biographical data, was a third unidentified man, another Mr. Nobody.

I picked up the telephone and called the mortuary. Seifel had just left there. He was a fourth.

CHAPTER
11

I heard him taking the steps two at a time, and opened the door. He was breathing hard, like a sprinter who had barely made it to the tape. His eyes had a glassy sheen and his face was loose, as if a heavy block of experience had fallen out of the California sky and struck him a dazing blow.

"You shouldn't do these things to me," he said in an unsuccessful attempt at lightness. "That room. That face. I'm a tenderly nurtured boy. I can't take death in the afternoon."

"Do you know the man?"

"I believe I do. I think I can say I'm virtually certain I've seen him. But lawyers make poor witnesses, you know—"

I interrupted his nervous wordiness: "Sit down and tell me about it."

"Yes, of course." His glance moved unsteadily around the dingy walls and rested on the sweet peas on Ann's desk. They were beginning to fade. "Say, old man, could I have a drink of some kind? My throat is parched."

I pointed to the cooler. "All we stock is water."

"Water will be fine. Adam's ale, my mother calls it." He filled and drained a paper cup, three times. "How in the world did you know I'd seen that chap?" he said with his back to me.

"That's beside the point. . . ."

"Was it dear little Annie?"

"We're wasting time. Now come in here and sit down and talk." I opened the door of the inner office and motioned him in.

He looked me sharp in the eye as he went by. His mouth still wet from his drink, his short hair bristling, he gave a sly and dangerous impression, like an animal caught in an alien corner of the woods. His short lip curled. "Do I detect a faintly peremptory note? Was that a sneer of cold command, Mr. Ozymandias?"

"Cut the comedy, Seifel. You could be in a jam."

"Don't be ridiculous," he said uneasily. "What has Annie been saying to you anyway? Hell hath no fury like a woman scorned."

Disregarding the question, I sat down behind my desk and put a fresh tape on the recording-machine.

He leaned across the desk, protesting. "What's that you're doing? You have no right to record what I say. You have no police powers."

"My office has investigative functions. I interpret them pretty broadly, and nobody seems to object. Do you object?"

"Naturally I object."

"Why?"

"I'm not prepared to make a formal statement. I've had an upsetting day, the sight of that body—"

"And you won't talk without advice of counsel. Why don't you widen that split in your personality and be your own counsel?"

He stiffened and grew pale. "I didn't come here to be insulted. As a matter of fact, I didn't like the way you asked me in the first place."

"Go back to your office and we'll start over. I'll send you a *billet-doux* pinned to an orchid."

He leaned close, supporting his weight on outspread palms: "I suspect you don't know who you're talking to, old man. I was light-weight champion at Stanford before the war. And if you weren't a friend of Annie's, I'd bat your ears off here and now. Just needle me a little more and I will anyway."

"If you're a friend of hers, speak of her with a little more respect. Her friends call her Ann, by the way."

He clenched his right fist. "You're asking for it, Cross."

"And you talk a good fight." I stood up, staring at him hard and level. I suspected that he was hollow or soft inside. Even his anger was a little actorish. His face and mouth made the motions and the sounds, but they didn't ring quite male. "Come down to the gym next week and I'll take you up on it. Right now I have other things on my mind."

I flicked the switch of the recorder. The twin spools began to revolve.

"Stop that thing," he said in a high-pitched voice. "I refuse to talk for the record."

"So you can change your story later on, when you've had more time to think? What's the matter, Seifel? You've got me half convinced that you're involved—"

"I could sue you for that!" He glared at the whirling spools. "If you play that tape with the accusation on it to one or more persons, you're actionable under the libel laws. I advise you to wipe it off."

"It's not recording yet. You have to press this button." I pressed it, and set the microphone on the desk between us. "Mr. Lawrence Seifel, interviewed by Cross, May 10th, four p.m. Sit down please, Mr. Seifel."

"I wish to state my objections to the recording of my statement at the present time." But he sat down. The machine between us enforced an impersonal atmosphere.

"What did you tell Lieutenant Cleat, Mr. Seifel?"

"Nothing. I told him, that is, that you had asked me to

look at the corpse. Nothing more. He seemed to be busy conferring with the sheriff's men, and you had emphasized the desirability of haste.''

''You recognized the corpse?''

He answered without hesitation: ''I did.''

''Who is he? Do you know his name?''

''Unfortunately I don't. He may have mentioned it to me, in fact I'm quite sure he did. My memory isn't too good for names, and I only met him the once.''

''When? On what occasion?''

''Just a minute. I could remember better, and express myself more freely, if you'd turn that instrument off.''

''Is that a threat to withhold information, Mr. Seifel?''

''Certainly not,'' he said emphatically, to the machine. ''It's a simple psychological fact, and I resent your attempt to ask tendentious and misleading questions of that nature.''

''Sorry, Mr. Seifel. You asked for it.''

''Will you turn it off?''

''I will not. You've just admitted that your memory is faulty, and I don't trust mine. . . .''

''I've admitted nothing of the sort. What is this, a cross-examination? I object to the whole procedure, on constitutional grounds.''

''Save it, this isn't a courtroom. I have to record your statement, it's too important not to. So far as we know, you're the only person in town who knows the deceased.''

''I don't know him. I only met him once.''

''This is where we came in. On what occasion did you meet him?''

''It was the day of Frederick Miner's trial, February the 20th, I believe it was. This man—the deceased—was present. I noticed him among the spectators. He was the only one I didn't know. There weren't many spectators—just the Johnsons, and Miner's wife, and one or two others—since it wasn't really a trial. All it amounted to was the guilty plea and the business of setting a date for Miner's probation hearing.''

"Mrs. Johnson was there?"

"Certainly."

"She said she'd never seen the man."

"Probably she didn't. He was sitting at the back of the well, apart from the others. I only noticed him on account of his bald head, you know how a bald head stands out. After court adjourned, I stayed behind for a few minutes. There were a few corrections I wanted the court reporter to make in the transcript. The bald-headed man waited for me at the back of the room. He buttonholed me on my way out.

"He was a pretty sordid-looking customer, as you know, and I tried to give him a quick brush-off. But he seemed to be very interested in the case. I gathered that he had followed it in the paper; he knew the names of the principals, my name, and Miner's, and the Johnsons'. I got the idea after a while. He came around to it rather circuitously. He wanted me to employ him."

"To do what?"

"That was never entirely clear. He claimed to be a detective, a private investigator of some sort, but I had my doubts about that. When I asked to see his credentials he ignored the request. I think he gave me some kind of card, though. Something with a Los Angeles address or telephone number."

"Do you still have it?"

"Perhaps I have. I haven't made a search."

"Where would it be?"

"In my office, if it's anywhere. I may have stuck it in among the papers in the Miner case. In fact, I probably did. I had them in my hand."

"If you did, it would certainly help. We could use a lead. About his name, the name he gave you—was it Kerry Smith?"

Seifel looked up at the ceiling, as if there might be a written clue on the plaster. The only clues there were the watermarks where the roof had leaked through two rainy seasons, before the Supervisors became officially aware of it.

"It wasn't Kerry Smith. I think it was a one-syllable surname, but no so common as Smith. Lint, or Kemp, something along those lines. And the first name definitely wasn't Kerry."

"He wanted you to hire him to do something, but you don't know exactly what?"

"That's right. He wasn't too easy to follow. He talked a great deal without saying much, praising his own discretion and general aptitude. In addition to which, he had a breath that kept me off. The stink of corruption. I was dodging his breath half the time, and only half-listening."

"He's not the only one who says very little at length."

He bridled. "If you mean me, the remark is definitely uncalled for. I've done my best to co-operate. I didn't expect my efforts to be appreciated."

"I'll write you a letter when I have the time. Surely you remember something of what he said?"

"I remember I didn't like it. If you want my subjective opinion, it crossed my mind at the time that he was trying to find an angle, a blackmailing angle."

"To blackmail you?"

"Certainly not." He laughed faintly and hollowly. "As near as I can recall, he wanted me, as Helen Johnson's lawyer, to persuade her to employ him as an investigator. He said he was sure he could discover the identity of Miner's hit-run victim, and that Mrs. Johnson might be interested."

"Was she?"

"I didn't discuss it with her. She had enough on her mind. One thing a lawyer can do is try to protect his clients against unsavory characters."

I switched off the tape recorder. "This protection service you give, could it include the use of an icepick, Seifel?"

He jumped in his chair. "Are you insane?"

"I'm asking the questions. Did you follow up the matter and find out that he knew something dangerous about Mrs. Johnson?"

"You are insane," he said. "I saw the man once, just once. I've volunteered my information—"

"Under considerable pressure."

He pulled at the button-down collar of his shirt. "You've got me all wrong. You've got Mrs. Johnson all wrong. I tell you Helen Johnson could no more have any connection with a man like that—" Seifel ran out of words. He stood up, his straightening legs pushing back the chair. "You can go to hell."

I got up, too. "Relax. You know as well as I do that questions have to be asked, if you want answers." I felt the faint beginnings of liking for Seifel. When he forgot himself, he had moderately decent instincts. I spoke to them: "If we don't solve this, Helen stands to lose most."

He pulled his hand down one side of his face in a weary gesture. "Ask me anything you like. I have nothing to hide. Neither has she. You don't know Helen Johnson."

"I have nothing against her." It was an understatement. "If you suspected attempted blackmail, why did you shake hands with the man? Tell him you'd look him up if you needed his help?"

"Annie's got you well primed, eh?"

"Leave Ann out of it. Answer the question."

"You're a darned unpleasant character to talk to, but I will. It's a way I have of dealing with people, I don't say it's a good way, but it's sort of a professional necessity with me. When I was a kid, and I hated a guy, I bopped him. Just like that. It got me into a lot of trouble. Nowadays I lean over backwards to be nice to them. The more I hate them, the nicer I treat them. I don't know why, it's just the way I operate. I hated that man."

"Why?"

"He represented pure evil to me." Seifel was speaking candidly at last, or acting much more expertly. The name of Helen Johnson had acted as a moral catalyst, or a stimulus to greater histrionic effort.

"I have a nose for evil," he continued. "I saw a lot of it

when I was a kid in Chicago in the twenties, and later when I was doing court-martial work for the Navy.''

"We have something in common after all."

He smiled rather tightly. "I'm willing to bet you've never been kidnapped. I was."

"You were kidnapped?"

"By my own father, when I was three years old. My mother had divorced him, and got custody of me. He came to our apartment one afternoon when my mother was out, and talked the maid into letting him take me for a walk. He was the sort of man who could talk the devil out of hell. He dropped out of sight with me for several days, before the police caught up with him. Of course I don't remember the incident, or my father either, but Mother's often told me about it."

"It wasn't a kidnapping for ransom?"

"No, of course not. All he wanted was me. The guy got a pretty rough deal when they caught him. Mother's family had a lot of pull in Illinois, and they had him committed to a mental hospital. She took back her maiden name, and changed my name to hers." He spoke rapidly, almost lightly, but he was pale with emotion. His tan was like a jaundice over the pallor. "I don't know why I'm telling you all this, Cross. I've never told it to anyone before."

"It's the room," I said. "It's heard a thousand confessions. I honestly think it induces them."

"Or you do," he said, smiling uneasily. "I wouldn't want that story to get around town, naturally."

"It won't. What was your father's name?"

"I have no idea. My mother's suppressed him completely, you understand. It's as if I had never had a father. All I know about him is that he was a young criminal-lawyer when they were married. Apparently he did something unethical, because he was disbarred. My mother divorced him on account of that, at least that's the reason she's always given me."

"Your mother must have very high ethical standards."

"She has. You might say my own career has been a reaction against his. Mother always steered me away from criminal law. I never touched it, except of course when I had to, in the Navy."

"Not all criminal lawyers are shysters."

"I know that. Clarence Darrow was my great hero when I was in law school. How did we get on all this? I started to explain about my nose for evil. Anyway, I have one. I could smell the odor of hellfire on that fellow in the courtroom."

I moved around him to the door. "Let's get over to your office and see if we can find his card."

"Whatever you say. Tom Swift and his jet-propelled pogo-stick are at your disposal."

Seifel's personality leaped back and forth among its multiple poles with the speed and dazzle of an electric arc. He was a hard man to keep track of.

CHAPTER
12

His office contrasted rather spectacularly with mine. We ascended into it in a small private hydraulic elevator whose door was finely lettered in gold with the firm name: Sturtevant and Seifel. Sturtevant, now semiretired, had been the town's leading estate-lawyer.

The reception room was carpeted with wine-dark broadloom and furnished with chartreuse leather. Reproduced Rouault heads looked out of the paneled walls in tragic resignation. There was nothing Rouault about the secretary at the telephone desk. She had wine-dark eyes and chartreuse hair, as if the room had given birth to her.

"Mrs. Seifel has been trying to get you, Mr. Seifel. Three times." She gave the words a sardonic intonation.

"What does Mother want now?"

"She says you promised to take her to a party at the beach club. You were to pick her up at four thirty."

"If she says that, it's probably true." There was an undertone of resentment in his voice. "Call her back please, will you, Linda? Tell her I'll be a little late."

"She won't like that."

He raised his bent arm in a violent, harried movement, and looked at his watch. "Tell her I'll be fifteen minutes late, no more. I don't see why she had to start so early."

"Yes, Mr. Seifel. Can I go then, Mr. Seifel? I have a beauty appointment."

"*I have a beauty appointment!*" he repeated in savage mimicry.

She stuck out her tongue at his back, caught me watching her, and substituted a feline smile. I followed Seifel into his private office, where the carpet and the leather were dove-gray, the paneling blanched oak. I remarked that law seemed to be paying well these days. He grunted unhappily that he supposed it was.

On the wall behind the black glass-topped desk, a bad oil-painting of a beautiful dark-haired woman in a 1920 cloche hat dominated the room. I guessed that it was Mrs. Seifel keeping an eye on her son. He opened a small bar-cabinet into a corner and held up a bottle of Scotch:

"Join me?"

"Not just now, thanks."

"I think I will." He added unnecessarily: "Though I very seldom drink in the daytime. Today is a special occasion. A kidnapping in the morning, a cocktail party with Mother in the afternoon. I couldn't face it without a little assistance. Not that she isn't a wonderful woman, of course."

He half-filled a glass with Scotch, and held it up to the painted face on the wall:

"Here's to you, Mother-Wother, in your home in the Sudan. You're a poor benighted heathen but a first-class fighting man."

There was something weirdly pathetic about the scene. Strangely, it was Ann I was sorry for. He tossed the whisky down.

"Now to find that card, wherever it is. Tom Swift and His X-ray Eye to the Rescue. Sequel to Tom Swift and His Electronic Mother-Wother."

He disturbed me. His wit was ranging on the borders of despair, and I regretted the crack I had made about split personality. He went on talking, more or less to himself, about the pleasures of the day and the delightful prospects of the evening, while his hands went through his files.

He slammed the metal drawer and turned with a card in his hand. "Just as I thought, old man. It was with the Miner papers. Little old Tom Swift has a memory like a steel trap, which is why the world has beaten a path to his door."

"Thank him for me."

The card was soiled and bent, as if it had been offered and rejected a number of times. It said:

ACME INVESTIGATIVE AGENCY
3489 Sunset Boulevard
Quickest Service, Lowest Rates
PHONE *TU-8-2181*

Seifel said: "I wish I could remember his name. Will this help, do you think?"

"It should. Mind if I use your phone for a long-distance call?"

"Any other time, no. Right now I'm in rather a hurry."

"It won't take long."

He hovered anxiously around the desk, like a large bird with clipped wings, while I put through a call to the

Tucker number. The phone at the other end rang twenty times.

"Your party does not answer, sir," the operator said. "Shall I try again in half an hour?"

"Don't bother."

Seifel accompanied me to the elevator. Just as we reached it, a metal door slid back and a woman emerged. At first glance, it was as if the portrait in Seifel's office had stepped down out of the frame. The dark aquiline head had remained unchanged for thirty years or more, and the body on which the head was balanced birdlike was as slim as a girl's.

At second glance I noticed the leathery patches loose under the jaw, the marks of old knowledge around the painted mouth and in the black, shining eyes. Her ringed hand took hold of Seifel's sleeve and gave it a violent jerk.

"What on earth has been keeping you, Lawrence?"

"I was just coming, Mother. This is Mr. Cross."

She disregarded me. Her eyes were on her son, like wet, black leeches. "It's mean and selfish of you to keep me waiting like this. I didn't devote my life to you in order to be cast aside whenever you feel the whim."

"I'm sorry, Mother."

"Indeed you should be sorry. You forced me to take a public bus down here."

"You could have taken a taxi."

"I can't afford to pay taxi-fare every day. You never think of my sacrifices, of course, but it has cost me an enormous amount of money to set you up in practice with Mr. Sturtevant."

"I realize that." He looked at me miserably. His body seemed to have shrunk, and taken on an adolescent awkwardness. "Can't we drop the subject for now, Mother? I'm ready to drive you anywhere you like."

She said with icy boredom: "Finish your business, Lawrence. I'm in no hurry. In fact I've lost any interest I had in the party. I believe I feel a headache coming on."

"Please, Mother, don't be like that."

He fumbled awkwardly, reaching for her hand. She turned away from him in a movement of disdainful coquetry, and walked to the window on high sharp heels. I stepped into the elevator. The last I saw of his face, it looked bruised and shapeless, as if her Cuban heels had been hammering it.

CHAPTER
13

Sam Dressen, the Sheriff's identification man, was in his cubicle in the courthouse. Lieutenant Cleat was a more efficient officer, but I was feeling a little soured on Cleat. Sam was biting on a hangnail, and his eyes were heavy with woe. His gray hair had been pulled and worried into spikes and whorls like a last-year's thistle patch.

Sighing with the effort, he lifted his eyes to the level of my face. "Hello, Howie. Two will get you twenty you dropped in to tell me what a flop I am. That's the big fad in law-enforcement agencies all over the country these days—telling Sam Dressen where to turn in. First the Chief lets me have it, then those goldarn federal—"

"Wait a minute, Sam. You're talking about the bureau I love. What's the trouble?"

"Job trouble. What other kind of trouble is there?"

"Woman trouble, for instance."

"Not at my age, boy. I got one and a half years to go for the County pension, and the whole gang of them want to cut me off from it. Everybody from J. Edgar Hoover down to the Chief are out to get me. You know that, Howie?"

"I hear you telling me."

"The Chief used to be my buddy, but he's a changed man. Ever since he took that course in F.B.I. School, he's so goldarn spit-and-polish you wouldn't recognize him. Know what he said to me today? He said if I don't brush up on my fingerprinting technique, he said he'd fire me, just like that." The old man tried to snap his fingers, unsuccessfully. "Me with eighteen years in the department, going on nineteen. They think I can afford to retire, on the salaries they pay?"

"What is it, Sam, a kickback on the February deal?"

He jerked at the hangnail with yellow teeth. "You heard about it, eh?"

"I heard they couldn't use the prints you took from that hit-run victim."

"That's right, they flung them back in my face, said they were too faint to classify."

"Were they?"

"I guess so, that's what they said, they're the experts." He looked at me from the corners of his vein-webbed eyes to see if I was with him. "You don't know the difficulties I was working under, Howie. Rigor mortis, and the stiff had awful faint markings, you could barely see them with the naked eye. All right, so I fluffed it. Everybody fluffs now and then. I'm only human like the rest of us. They didn't have to write that snooty letter to the Chief. What does it matter who the guy was? He's dead."

"It's beginning to look as if it might be important, Sam. I'm thinking of asking for an exhumation order."

"On account of the killing this morning? You think there's a tie-up?"

"That's the general idea."

"Well, don't expect me to know nothing about it. I just went over to take a look at that new stiff, and the morgue was crawling with federal men. They wouldn't even let me near it, said they were handling the identification routine themselves. How do you like that, Howie?"

Since Sam had been slipping for a year or more, I liked it

fairly well. On the other hand he was an old friend, and a useful one. I made a sympathetic noise in the back of my throat.

He wasn't consoled. "So the Chief bawls me out all over again. I made him lose face, he said. I said if I had a face like that, I wouldn't mind losing a piece of it—"

"You said that?"

"Not out loud, I didn't. Under my breath. I wouldn't be sitting here now if I said it out loud. I got a pension to protect. But it don't look as if I'm going to make it." He sighed like a wind-broken horse. "Well, what is it you want, Howie? You never come over to bat the breeze any more unless you want something."

"I have something for you." I took the bent businesscard out of my wallet and laid it on the desk under his melancholy nose. "This belonged to the man in the mortuary. He gave it to Larry Seifel in February." I described the circumstances briefly. "Show it to the Sheriff. It should do his face some good. Tell him to get a statement from Seifel. You know Seifel?"

"Sure I know him. He's another," he said obscurely. "There's two kinds of young twerps. He's the kind with no respect for their elders, he'd push an older man right out of the picture to make room for himself. You're the other kind, Howie," he added as an afterthought.

"Did you have trouble with Seifel?"

"No trouble, he can't make trouble for me. But he was in last week, fretting about that body in the Miner case. I'm sorry I ever heard of the Miner case."

"You're going to hear more, I'm afraid. What did he want?"

"Information. I told him I didn't have any new information. He seemed to think I should have. Shucks, I got more to think about than that one case. That armed-robbery gang we nabbed on Tuesday, there's inquiries on 'em from six states, fourteen police departments. I'm over my ears in paperwork." He grabbed a wad of papers from his in-basket and slammed it down in front of him.

"Forget about them for now. Just what information do you have, Sam?"

"Nothing new. I followed down a lead this week. It turned out to be a dead end. It was the last decent lead I had—the cleaner's mark on the suit the guy was wearing."

"No maker's label?"

"The maker's label had been removed. Know why? The suit was stolen. I found out that much."

"Go on."

"This cleaner is in Westwood. It's a new business, just started last year, and independent, so it wasn't so easy to trace. Missing Persons didn't even have it on file. Anyway, I finally got a chance to go up to L.A. on Wednesday—I had some stuff to deliver to Ray Pinker. The cleaner gave me the name and address of the people the suit was stolen from. I didn't know at the time the suit was stolen, though. I thought I was getting somewhere."

I was getting impatient. The afternoon was fading toward its close, and I was wasting what was left of it. "What did you find out, Sam? You interviewed the people it was stolen from?"

"I tried to. They weren't home. I talked to the maid on the telephone from the cleaner. I described the suit. She said it was stolen, along with a lot of other loot, about four months ago. So apparently the guy was a burglar. Anyway, it explains what he was doing out on Ridgecrest Road that night, probably casing a joint he was going to rob. When Miner run him down, he did somebody a big favor."

"Give me the name and address."

"What name and address? I just got finished telling you it was a dead end."

"The people the suit was stolen from. I'm going to Westwood and talk to them."

"What's the use? They never caught the burglar."

"Any lead is better than none. Let's have it, Sam."

"Sure, if you want to go to all that trouble." He rummaged in an overflowing drawer, and came up with a cleaner's invoice blank on which he had written in pencil:

> *J. Thomas Richards*
> 8 Juncal Place
> Westwood

"Better warn them you're coming," Sam said. "It's a long way to drive for nothing, and they're gallivanters."

"I'll do that. There's one more thing."

"Aren't we even yet?" He bared his teeth in a shrewd smile. "Want me to throw in the shirt off my back?"

I pretended not to notice the needle. The old man had been having a hard day. "The Sheriff will sit up and beg when you show him that card. You'll give it to him right away?"

"As soon as I get the heck rid of you, Howie."

"That won't be hard. All I want is the pictures you took of Miner's victim."

"They're not supposed to go out of here, you know that."

"I promise to bring them back."

"You think you can establish identification?"

"I'm going to try. If I do, you get first crack at it."

"I'll take your word on that, Howie. I don't think you can do it, though, unless you got a tip I don't know about." His wrinkled smile was like an old scar that still hurt sometimes. There was a time when Sam had hoped to be sheriff.

"Set your mind at rest. I haven't. Let's have the pictures, Sam."

He unlocked a green metal cabinet against the wall, and pawed the dark shelves. A shaft of sunlight, almost horizontal, thrust through the tall barred window behind his desk. In the faint and broken sunlight, his searching profile was dark and poignant. It was like an old stone face roughed and eroded by too many rainy seasons.

"Don't worry, Sam," I said in a low voice that he could choose not to hear. "You'll make your pension."

He found the folder he was looking for, and opened it on the desk. I had my first look at the face of the first anonymous man. He had probably been younger and better-looking than the second, the one in the mortuary, but that was before Miner's car has smashed his features. They were badly damaged; jaw dislocated, nose flattened, cheeks and brow abraded, one eye gone. The one good identifying feature was the light wavy hair grow in low and thick on the cut forehead.

"The impact bust the fog lamp," Sam was saying. "Both the wheels passed over him. Caved his chest in, cracked his skull like a pecan, drove the glass into his face."

"Blond hair?"

"That's right. Gray-blue eyes. Five nine, about one sixty, twenty-nine or thirty. The way I reconstruct him, he was a nice-looking boy."

"Special characteristics?"

"Just this." He turned over to a closeup of an arm, captioned "Left Forearm." It was tattooed with a hula girl wearing a lei, and the word *Aloha*. "I figure he was in the Navy, probably. Too bad he didn't have his serial number tatooed on him."

He closed the manila folder and tied it with tape. It took him quite a long time, because his hands were shaking.

"Feeling all right, Sam?"

"I'm all right. It's just these bodies get me down, lately even the pictures get me down. I know darn well I fluffed this print job last February. It was terrible, Howie. I couldn't hardly bring myself to handle him. It's a rough experience for an old guy like me to see any young fellow cut off. It makes you think dark thoughts, boy, it does me anyway." His large bony hand clutched my arm and held on desperately. "Am I losing my grip, Howie?"

"We're all afraid of death," I said. "It's normal to be afraid."

"Don't say that word, Howie. I can't stand to hear that

word. I seen so many of them. I only realized the last couple of years that any day now it's going to be me.''

"Morbid thoughts," I said cheerfully as I went out. But they trailed my car like black crepe all the way to Los Angeles. I drove as if death were behind me on a motorcycle.

CHAPTER
14

The Acme Investigative Agency had second-floor offices in a narrow, stucco building above a loan company. I found a parking place across the street and made my way through the evening flow of traffic. The cars were fleeing wildly across the twilight, as if there had been simultaneous disasters at both ends of the boulevard. Lights were being lit like tiny watchfires all along the hills.

I walked up to the second floor and found, as I expected, that the Acme offices were locked and silent. There was a telephone booth which smelled of stale cigar-smoke in the corridor. A skylight above it filtered a dusty gray light. I used the phone to call the J. Thomas Richards home in Westwood. The maid informed me that Mr. and Mrs. Richards were still out on the golf course. Would I try the Bel Air clubhouse? Yes, they were expected home for dinner.

The telephone directory chained to the wall of the booth listed an alternative number for the Acme agency, to be called in case of emergency. I dialed it and got a man's voice, rapid and edged:

"Bourke speaking. Is that you, Carol?"

"I'm Howard Cross, probation officer in Pacific Point—"

"Do I know you?"

"It looks as if you're going to. We've had a murder and a kidnapping—"

"Not for me, thanks very much. I leave that stuff to the police. Who did you say you were—a probation officer?"

"You didn't let me finish. You run the Acme agency, don't you?"

"It runs me," he said, "ragged."

"One of your employees is involved."

"Simmie? Not Simmie Thatcher?"

"We don't know the name."

"He won't talk?"

"He can't. He's been dead for eight hours."

He didn't speak for about five seconds. Somewhere behind the wall of the corridor, perhaps in the Acme office, I heard a telephone ringing remotely, unanswered.

"What makes you think he works—he worked for me?"

"He was passing out your business cards."

"Describe him."

"A big old man, close to six feet, I'd say in his late fifties. Bald-headed, and he wears a brown toupee."

There was another waiting silence on the line.

"Do you know him, Bourke?"

"I know him," he said wearily. "What happened to him?"

"He was murdered."

"I see."

"Who is he?"

"The name's Art Lemp. He worked for me last year for a while. I fired him."

"I need all you have on him. Where can we get together?"

"Now?" he said in some dismay. "I'm expecting a call from my wife, I can't—"

I overbore him: "Listen. This Lemp snatched a four-year-old boy this morning. Lemp's dead. The boy's still missing. You're the only lead we've got."

"I see. Well. Maybe she isn't going to call me anyway. Where are you?"

"In the telephone booth outside your office."

"I'm just three blocks away. Be there in five minutes."

Before I had finished a cigarette he mounted the stairs, a man of about my age, broad-shouldered and short-legged, with quick suspicious Hollywood eyes set on ball bearings in an anxious face. While we exchanged a perfunctory handshake his eyes were all over me, estimating my height, age, weight, probable income, and Intelligence Quotient. There were Martinis on his breath.

He stabbed his office door with a small brass key. "Did I keep you waiting? Mind if I see your credentials?"

"I don't carry any. Phone the sheriff at Pacific Point if you like. He's probably been trying to get in touch with you, anyway."

He snapped a switch inside the door. The awkward shadows of waiting-room furniture, settee, reed chairs, ashstand, took on color and substance.

"Why bother?" he said with forced lightness. "You have an honest face. What did you say your name was?"

"Howard Cross."

"Come on into the sanctum, Howard. I'll do you for what I can. Joke."

I followed him into his private office, a small room decently furnished in oak veneer. He sat on the edge of the desk and swung one highly polished toe.

"Frankly, this comes as a blow to me, Howard. Been taking quite a series of them lately. Wife left me, third time. Been trying to talk her into coming back. Big showdown scheduled for tonight. Isn't that the irony of fate, Howard? Me in the divorce business, knocking myself out to keep a no-good blonde from leaving me. Sure, you say, let her go. Only she has what I need."

"Pin up the back hair, Bourke. I'm interested in Lemp, not you."

"Sorry," he said, not without resentment. "What happened to old Art? Shot? I always told him he was going to get shot."

"Icepicked. He was murdered in his car about eleven fifteen this morning, apparently hijacked for the ransom money. He'd just picked it up at eleven."

"How much ransom money?"

"Fifty thousand."

Bourke narrowed his eyes and pinched his lips between thumb and forefinger. He looked like a hungry barracuda wearing a bowtie. "Old Art tried the big time, eh? He shouldn't have done that. He had no class. Naturally he got it in the neck."

"In the neck?"

"Excuse my slang," he said. "Don't tell me that's where he took the icepick."

"That's where."

"Shut my big mouth, eh? But you're way off the beam if you think I knew about it. I haven't even seen Art Lemp for six months. I fired him in December. As a matter of fact, I kicked him downstairs."

"Why?"

"The urge kept growing on me, it finally bust loose. I never should have hired him in the first place. Only did it as a favor to a pal."

"What pal?"

The barracuda eyes grew wary. "Aren't we getting kind of far afield, Howard?"

"I don't think so. Lemp wasn't alone in this. I'm trying to contact his associates."

"You have a point. Well, it wasn't exactly a pal that steered him to me, not my pal anyway. A little blonde chick name of Molly Fawn, at least that's the name she uses. She's done me a couple of favors in the past. When she told me about this deserving old goat with all the police experience, I broke down and gave him a job."

"When was this?"

"October, early October. It took me two months to catch on to him. He wouldn't have lasted that long if Carol hadn't been driving me off my rocker. She left me the second time in November. Can I help it if I have contacts with women in my business? I told her I'm like a doctor, she wouldn't listen. I never gave that—'' he snapped his fingers loudly— ''for Molly Fawn or any of the rest of them.''

''Where can I get in touch with Molly Fawn?''

His face expressed regretful concern. ''I'll be honest with you, Howard.''

''Don't strain yourself.'' I was always suspicious of people who made a point of proclaiming their honesty.

Leaning forward, Bourke slapped my shoulder heartily and laughed with his teeth. ''No strain, I'm leveling with you, don't get me wrong. I haven't laid an eye on Molly this year. I broke with her and Lemp at the same time, for the same reason. I'll even tell you the reason.'' He looked sideways in surprise at his own generous candor. ''They were using the leads Lemp got working for me, to run a little sideshow of their own.''

''Blackmail?''

''It boiled down to that. I get a lot of jealous wives in here.'' He sniffed with distaste, as if female emotions had left traces in the room. ''A fair percentage of them have nothing to be jealous about. It's my job to set their minds at rest as soon as I can. Art Lemp was assigned to two or three of these cases. He played them the opposite way, for maximum trouble—a variation on the badger game. Twice that I know about, he maneuvered the husband into a compromising position with Molly, once in a car, once in a hotel room. Then this photographer pal of his took a picture. One of the suckers bought the picture from Lemp. What would you do if you had a jealous wife? The other one came to me. That was the day I kicked Art Lemp downstairs.'' A reminiscent smile twitched at the corners of his mouth. ''I phoned Molly and gave her a tongue-lashing, and I haven't seen her since, either. If it wasn't so bad for business, I'd have marched the two of them down to the station-house.''

''Where was Molly living in December?''

"I don't know where she lived."

"Try her phone number."

"I never knew her phone number."

"You said you phoned her."

"Through a friend," he said, with an explanatory lifting of the hands. "She had an arrangement with this friend of hers to handle her phone calls for her."

"Her friend should know where she is."

"That I doubt. The friend in question is serving time in the L.A. County Jail. The Vice Squad put her away in January. Maybe they got Molly, too. I couldn't care less."

"Lemp had a nice circle of friends," I said, thinking that Bourke had, too. "What about the photographer you mentioned, the one that took the compromising pictures?"

"I never met him. I'd have fixed him if I had. Don't even know his name."

"Or where he lived?"

"I think he lived in the same hotel with Lemp, one of those crummy joints downtown. That was where they took one of the pictures."

"The Sunset Hotel?"

"You're getting psychic, Howard."

"The car Lemp was killed in belonged to a Kerry Smith, who gave the Sunset Hotel as his address. Does the name Kerry Smith mean anything to you?"

"Not a thing. If he's the flashbulb boy, he probably isn't there any more. Lemp checked out in December, the day I gave him the stairs treatment. Flashbulb probably went along with him."

"You have no description of the photographer?"

"Not a thing," he repeated. "I can give you a good one of Molly Fawn, if you want. Fawn isn't her real name, incidentally—just a stage name."

"Is she an actress?"

"They're all actresses, Howard. Every female bum in town is an actress, if all they did was gallop in the second line of a third-rate nitery in San Francisco. Just like half the male bums call themselves artists and writers. And private investigators." He smiled wryly.

"Molly's description," I reminded him.

"You've seen a hundred of her, Howard, maybe a thousand in your work. Well-turned little blonde, of course not natural blonde, height about five feet four, weight about one twenty-five, good legs but they could be better. Claims to be nineteen or twenty. One thing, if you catch up with her, don't believe anything she says. She's a psychopathic liar. They're all psychopathic liars. I know, I'm married to one."

"You could be prejudiced. Color of eyes?"

"Pansy-purple, I mean the flower. Her eyes are her best feature, and she knows it. Used them all the time, on everything in trousers."

"Distinguishing characteristics?"

"None that I know of. She has a very good skin. Funny thing about her, she doesn't tan." His voice dropped meditatively. "Funny thing."

On the desk behind him, the phone rang in sharp remonstrance. Bourke pivoted and lifted the receiver. "Carol? Is that you, baby?"

It wasn't Carol.

"Yes, Mr. Forest," he said. "This is Bourke speaking. Yes, I run the Acme Agency."

He answered a series of questions about Art Lemp, and then my name came up. Bourke handed me the receiver. "F.B.I. man, wants to talk to you."

Forest's voice came rasping over the long wire. "You've got the jump on us, I see. Don't fall and break your neck."

"I never have. Any news on the Johnson boy?"

Bourke, who had started to pace, froze in a listening attitude.

"We're combing the entire Southwest," Forest said. "Roadblocks on every highway out of the state. One definite lead: the Chrysler you found Lemp in was bought off a Third Street lot in December by a man named Kerry Snow.

Checks with Kerry Smith. No description, but we have a line on the salesman that sold it to him. What's at your end?''

"Bourke here put me onto a friend of Lemp's, a girl named Molly Fawn. You'd better come and talk to Bourke yourself."

"I intend to. Can he be trusted?"

"For our purposes, I'd say yes. He's right beside me."

"Send him out of the room."

"It's his room. He seems legitimate."

"Thank you veddy much," Bourke said at my back.

Forest was saying, darkly: "You never can tell about these private operators. The dirt they work in is always rubbing off on them. Well, put him back on the line, will you please?"

Bourke answered further questions, about himself and Molly Fawn and Lemp. Finally, I gathered, he was instructed to wait in his office for Forest. He promised to, and hung up.

The dialogue with authority had sobered and tired him, deepening the worry lines in his face. "He wants you to wait, too, Mr. Cross."

"I don't think I will. You'd better."

"More woe," he said lugubriously. "I haven't had a piece of luck this year. My luck's got to turn some time. You know this Forest?"

"I talked to him today. He's not going to bite you."

"That's what you think. I'm in this thing up to my eyes." He raised a stiff left hand to his left cheekbone. "You didn't tell me it was the Johnson kid."

"I didn't know you'd be interested."

"I'm not. I want to forget it. I want to get out in the desert and crawl in a gopher hole and forget everything. Only I can't."

"Let's have the rest of it, Bourke. You might as well."

"Don't worry. You don't catch me concealing evidence."

"Blurt it out," I said. "You're wasting time."

He circled the desk and sat down weakly in the swivel chair behind it. "This Johnson dame a friend of yours?"

"I wouldn't say that."

"I know her. Know her husband, that is. He was one of my clients. What's the old guy's name?"

"Abel. He isn't so old."

"Too old for her. That's not my opinion, it's his. He came in here six-seven months ago, caught my ad in the paper. I told you about the jealous wives. There are also the jealous husbands."

A whistling wind swept the region behind my eyes. In the ensuing blankness, something heavy and solid gathered. It felt like a headache. Then I discerned that it was shaped like a woman. But its face was blank, and its lower half was hidden.

"Go on." My voice sounded strange in the blankness. The shape turned its face to the back wall of my mind. "Who was he jealous of?"

"Some lawyer, a guy called Siphon, something like that. I could look it up."

"Don't bother. The name is Seifel."

He slanted a wise look at me. "Johnson didn't make any accusations. He said he just wanted to know, one way or the other. The doubt was killing him, he said. It always is."

"Did you settle his doubts?"

"I thought I did. Now I'm not so sure. Lemp was the one who handled it, see. As a matter of fact, he asked me to put him on the case, he seemed to be interested in it. I was busy myself on a studio job, and so were my other operators. I sent him down to Pacific Point. He watched the Johnson dame for four or five days. This was in November. He reported nothing there. Mrs. Johnson saw the legal eagle a couple of times but there was always a third party present, Johnson or the guy's mother. I'm no jackal: I told Johnson he was wasting his money."

"But now you're not so sure."

I tried to keep emotion out of my voice, but Bourke had a delicate ear for that sort of thing. "Don't get mad at me. I got enough people made at me already." He raised his bent right arm as if to ward off a series of looping left hooks. "Okay, so you like the lady. Look at the thing dispassionately. I know now, I didn't know then. Lemp's reports aren't worth the paper they're written on. Even if he caught them *in flagrante*, he wouldn't report it to me. He saw a chance for something bigger there: he must have been planning this snatch since November, maybe before I assigned him to the case. So he wouldn't do anything to precipitate trouble in the family. Would he?"

"I'd like to see his report."

Bourke pulled open a drawer in a filing-cabinet. He riffled through the papers in the drawer, casually at first, then more and more intently. "It isn't here. Lemp must have lifted it before he left."

"You're sure?"

"Look for yourself. This is all there is." He showed me a record of payment: Abel Johnson, Pacific Point, $125.00, for services rendered. "Forest is going to like this, very much."

He collapsed in the swivel chair and lifted a revolver from the middle drawer of the desk. Absently, he twirled the loaded chamber with his forefinger:

"Russian roulette, anyone?"

"Put it away," I said.

"R.K.O." He replaced the gun in the drawer. "Don't mind me, Howard. I was just kidding. I'm a great kidder."

"This is no time for comedy. If you know something more than you've told me, you'd better let me have it."

"Such as?"

"Where Molly Fawn lived. I think you knew her pretty well at one time. It's possible you still do."

"You're wrong, you couldn't be wronger." His face was expressionless, but below the edge of the desk his hands were wrestling quietly with each other. "I haven't seen that little twist since December."

"Where did you see her?"

He countered with a question: "Is she involved in this snatch?"

"She's involved with Lemp, and he's the key man in it. I shouldn't have to tell you this: your only chance of keeping yourself clear is to talk and talk some more."

His right hand bent his left hand backward onto his knee and vanquished it. "I visited her a couple of times in her apartment. She probably isn't there any more, but maybe she left a forwarding address. Anyway, you can try it. It's in West Hollywood." He gave me the address, and instructions for finding it.

"Thanks, Bourke. But why the long delay in spilling it?"

"I think she's San Quentin quail." He slapped himself across the eyes with his open left palm. "I must be nuts, I know what I ought to do every time, and half the time I can't do it. Maybe I'm just another bum."

I left him.

CHAPTER
15

The apartment was over an attached garage on a quiet rundown residential street. Its windows were dark, but there were lights and sounds in the adjoining house. It was a white frame bungalow whose lines aspired, rather feebly, to Colonial. The sounds inside were radio voices. When I rang the front-door bell, the voices were cut off suddenly, and soft slow footsteps approached the door.

The door was opened about four inches, on a chain. Spectacled eyes looked down a long female nose at me. A disapproving mouth said: "You've interrupted my favorite program. You'd think I had the right to some peace. What is it you want?''

"I'm sorry. The matter is urgent. I'm trying to find a girl who calls herself Molly Fawn.''

Her disapproval hardened, descending over her long face like an icecap. "I know nothing whatever about her. If you're another one of her worthless friends—''

"I'm a probation officer," I said, before she could close the door. "I'm investigating a very serious case.''

The icecap thawed perceptibly. Something that might have been pleasure glinted behind the spectacles. "Is she in trouble? I told that girl that she was heading for trouble, with her carryings-on. Why, when I was her age, I wasn't allowed to *speak* to a man. Father was strict with we girls—''

"May I come in?''

She unhooked the chain and opened the door another foot, just wide enough for me to squeeze through. "Promise you won't notice the condition of the house.''

The house was very clean, and preternaturally neat, like a barracks awaiting inspection. But everything in it was old: the carpeting, the furniture, even the outdated calendar in the hallway. The air in the living-room was stale and heavy, laden with an odor like musty spice. A faded motto on the wall above a closed upright piano stated: "The smoke ascends as lightly from the cottage hearth as from the haughty palace.''

She said, when she saw me reading it: "A great truth, isn't it? Would you like to sit down, Mr.—?''

"Cross, Howard Cross.''

"I am Miss Hilda Trenton. Happy to make your acquaintance, Mr. Cross.''

We sat in facing platform-rockers in front of the old cabinet radio. It was still lighted and humming like a repressed desire. Miss Trenton leaned towards me, sharp elbows on sharp knees: "What has she done?''

"I'm trying to find out. I take it she doesn't live here any more.''

"She was only here for a month or so, and I can tell you I wouldn't rent her the apartment again if she came to me on bended knee." She smiled grimly. "Of course she won't. She left owing a week's rent—decamped one day while I was at work without a by-your-leave. I was glad to see her go, to tell you the truth. I have a very nice young couple in the apartment now."

"When did she leave?"

"It was early in January, I don't remember the exact date."

"And naturally she didn't give you a forwarding address."

"I should say not. She still owes me eighteen dollars. I was foolish to trust her, even for a single week. Molly was full of stories, how her ship was due to come in any day. She was going to get a movie job and be a star and pay me double for waiting. Or else she was going to get married to a wonderful young man." She sniffed. "No decent young man would marry *her*."

"Why not?"

"She was morally loose, that's why. I saw her company, *masculine* company, at all hours of the day and night. It's a good thing she left when she did. I was thinking about evicting her." She patted the thin gray hair on top of her head. "But I let my charitable impulses get the better of me. I'm always doing that, Mr. Cross. People take advantage of it. It's my great vice."

"You say she took off in a hurry. Did she leave anything behind?"

She thought about it. "Not a thing, not a single, solitary thing." Miss Trenton was not a good liar. The shortsighted eyes behind the spectacles became suffused with moisture, and she coughed. "The apartment is completely furnished, you see. All she brought was her clothes."

I said with all the impressiveness I could muster:

"I know you're an upright citizen, Miss Trenton. I can rely on you to keep this to yourself. Molly Fawn is involved in a kidnapping case. If you know of any clue to her whereabouts, her personal life, her connections, it's your duty to let us know.''

"Kidnapping! How dreadful!" She hugged her shoulders, and looked at the door and windows of the room. "I haven't the faintest notion, haven't seen or heard of her since January. Now her personal life, that's another matter. She carried on something fierce with her men friends. There was dancing and parties in the apartment all hours of the night. And the things they said to each other!"

"You could hear them?"

"Well, I keep my car in the garage underneath. Some nights when I'd get home from work I'd be sitting in my car, trying to gather up enough energy to come into the house—I couldn't *help* but hear them. Other times when I was up in the attic, looking for something—well, the partition is thin, just one thickness of wallboard. I heard their nasty stories and talk. It grieved me to the bone to hear a young girl go on like that." She broke off and stared at her feet, which were shod in sensible black oxfords. If she felt grief, it was probably for herself.

"Did you see the men?"

"The stairs are on the other side of the garage. She generally smuggled them in and out when I wasn't looking."

"You must have seen their cars."

"I don't know a thing about cars. I'm still driving Father's old Ford."

"Perhaps you heard—overheard some of their names?"

She leaned her head to one side, one forefinger pressed into the hollow of the cheek. "There was a man called Art," she said after a while. "Molly didn't use his last name, just Art or Artie. They fought like cats and dogs when he came, called each other bad names—names I wouldn't soil my tongue with."

"What were they fighting about?"

"I could hardly tell. I didn't listen, you see, it's just what I overheard, accidentally."

"Of course."

"He kept wanting her to go away with him. She wouldn't go. She said he couldn't offer her enough to make it worth her while, that she had better prospects. Besides, she was always saying he was a crook. I tell you, Mr. Cross, it was terrible to have to listen to. The other fellow sounded much nicer to me. Not *nice*, but nicer."

"Other fellow?"

"The younger one, the one that came most often. He had a lovely voice, I'll say that for him." The eyes behind the spectacles grew soft with reminiscence, as if the unknown voice had been speaking to her, wooing her subtly through the attic wallboard. "*They* had their arguments, too, but with Kerry it was the other way around. She wanted him to marry—"

"Kerry?" I said.

"Did I say Kerry? It must have just slipped out. That was his name, at least the name she called him."

"Kerry Snow?"

"I never knew his last name. They were on a first name basis."

"I gathered that. What did they talk about?"

"Themselves. Each other. He was always saying he'd never trust a woman. She always claimed to be different. Then he'd make fun of her, and start her crying. I almost felt sorry for her sometimes."

I said: "Miss Trenton, as a woman of the world you won't object to my asking: were they living together?"

"Certainly not! I'd never permit such a thing in my apartment. Sometimes he stayed all night, of course. They'd talk all night." She added hastily: "I suffer from insomnia, I couldn't help hearing them."

"Did you ever see this Kerry?"

"Once or twice I did, at least I think it was him. I saw him sneaking out in the morning. I'm an early riser, I have to be. I'm due at the office every morning at five to eight, and it's halfway across town—"

"Can you describe him?"

"He's young, not over thirty I'd say. I suppose some women would consider him attractive, if you like that type of good looks. He has blondish hair, sort of wavy over the forehead, and nice clean-cut features if it wasn't for the sneaky look. He's a well-built young man, I'll say that for him."

"You must have seen his car, Miss Trenton. Think about it, now."

She screwed up her eyes and mouth in concentration: the wrinkled face was like a little girl's cartooned by time. "It was a big car, I noticed that, blue in color, I believe."

"What year?"

"Well, it wasn't new. It still looked pretty good."

"Would you know a Chrysler?"

"No," she said. "I never did know the different makes of cars. It was some kind of sedan, I remember that."

"Take your time now, Miss Trenton. See if you can dredge up any more facts about Kerry."

"Is he a kidnapper?"

"Very likely," I said, though I doubted it. More likely Kerry had been underground since February. "You sit and see what you can remember. There's something in my car I want to show you."

On the way back in through the hallway with my briefcase, I found that I didn't want to enter the living-room again. Its air, laden with faint mustiness and fainter spice, was like an Egyptian tomb where a little life stirred horribly under the windings. I went in anyway. Miss Trenton was rocking placidly. There was something black and oblong in her lap.

"I remembered *something*, Mr. Cross. She did leave something behind her after all. Don't you consider I have a right to it, with her owing me rent?"

"It depends on what it is."

She hefted the black object in her hands. "This camera. She left it in the linen closet, but it's possible it wasn't hers. I remember one day her friend Kerry was taking pictures of her in the driveway. She was in one of those strapless bathing-suits, on a Sunday. Soon as I saw what was going on in my driveway, I ordered them inside, I can tell you.''

I took the camera out of its case. It was worn but fairly good, worth perhaps a hundred dollars new. What interested me most about it was the legend stamped on the case in small gold letters: U.S.S. *Eureka Bay*. The camera itself bore a U.S. Navy serial number.

''This looks like Government property, Miss Trenton.''

''I didn't mean to keep it,'' she said quickly. ''What was I to do with it? Molly left it behind her, I didn't know where she went. I thought I'd just hold on to it until somebody came to claim it. That's perfectly legitimate—''

''Did Molly have a friend named Fred? Fred Miner?''

''I don't recollect that name.'' Her hands were covertly wiping themselves on her skirt, as if to remove all traces of the camera. ''You've asked me so many questions, my brain's in a whirl.''

''Fred is a heavily built man in his thirties, very broad in the shoulders. He has a stiff back. It was broken in the war. He wears old khaki uniforms most of the time. He has rather a large head with heavy features, big jaw and a thick nose, sandy hair cut short, gray eyes. Deep bass voice, Midwestern accent. Fred likes to use Navy slang.''

''Kerry did, too,'' she said unexpectedly. ''Kerry talked like a sailor. I wish I could remember some of the things he said—like calling the floor a deck, things like that.''

''What about Fred Miner?''

''There wasn't anybody answering his description. That doesn't say he wasn't here. I had better things to do than check up on Molly Fawn, remember that. Anything I heard or saw, it was practically forced on me.''

''I understand that, Miss Trenton. It's been very good of you to put up with all these questions. There's one more thing I'd like you to do. I have some pictures here, pictures of a man which were taken after the man's death. Are you willing to look at them, for identification purposes?''

''I guess so,'' she faltered, ''if it's important.''

I laid the photos of Miner's victim one by one in her hands. She peered down at them through her spectacles.

"It's Kerry," she said in a muffled voice. "I do believe it's Kerry."

"Are you sure?"

"Yes. I noticed the tattoo mark on his arm, that Sunday he was taking the pictures. But I don't understand. You said he was one of the kidnappers. Is he dead?"

"He's dead."

"Then he isn't one of the criminals you're after?"

"Not any more. He was run over by a car."

"Isn't that a shame. And here I was thinking he might come back any day to claim his camera."

"I'm going to have to take the camera with me."

"You're welcome *to* it." She rose suddenly, brushing her skirt with her hands, and cried out angrily: "I don't care for any souvenirs of *that* girl and her friends, thank you. It was good riddance of bad rubbish."

I said: "Good night. Don't bother to let me out."

"Good night."

She turned the radio up. Before I started my motor, I could hear the voices bawling and lamenting in her house.

CHAPTER
16

Juncal Place was high on a terraced hill overlooking the Westwood campus. It was a dead-end street one block long, with houses on the higher side and a steep drop on the other. The eighth and last house was set far back on a sloping lawn that ended above the sidewalk in stone retaining-walls cut by concrete stairs. It was a pseudo-Tudor mansion with dark oak facing, drooping eaves, and leaded panes in the second-story windows. Knocking on the grandiose oak front door, I felt a little like a character in *Macbeth*.

A colored maid in uniform opened the door and looked down at my briefcase with suspicion.

"Is Mr. Richards home?"

"I don't know. What is it you want?"

"Tell him it's about the burglary."

"Are you from the police?"

"I'm connected with the police."

"Why didn't you say so? Come in. I guess he'll see you."

She left me in a room with a heavily beamed ceiling and book-lined walls. Many of the books were beautifully bound, but they looked as if they had never been read. Someone had probably bought them all at once, stacked them in the cases because the room required them, and then forgotten them.

A round-faced white-haired man in a dinner jacket darted in, leaning forward as if the floor were slanted to his disadvantage. He shook my hand vigorously. "Glad to meet you, sergeant, always glad to meet a member of your fine organization. Magnificent library I have here, eh? Cost me five thousand dollars for the books alone. Wish I had time to read them. That organ in the alcove cost three five. Sit down. Can I offer you a drink?"

"No thanks. I'm not a detective, by the way. I'm a probation officer. The name is Cross."

"I see," he said uncomprehendingly. "I'm a great admirer of the work you boys are doing. Have a cigar?"

"No, thanks."

He clipped a long pale-green cigar and thrust the end into his mouth. "You don't know what you're missing," he said around it. "I have them specially made for me in Cuba. Cost me four fifty a thousand. I smoke a thousand of them in two months. You'd think it would spoil my condition but it doesn't. Matter of fact, I broke eighty today, for the eleventh time. Collected a little side-bet of two hundred dollars."

"Good for you, Mr. Richards."

The irony was lost on him. He beamed. "I'm no Bobby Jones. But I do make enough on my game to pay my club dues. The way it works out, I get all that fine exercise for nothing. Not to mention all the fine personal contacts." He lit his cigar, smacking his lips as he puffed, and blinked at me through the smoke. "You came about the burglary, Leah said. You haven't recovered the rest of our stuff?"

"I'm afraid not. I came on the chance that you could give me some information."

"About the stuff?"

"About the burglar," I said, but he wasn't listening.

He said: "The insurance company paid me off in full, you'll be glad to know. An aggregate of four hundred and twenty dollars. That included three hundred and forty dollars for the suit. They didn't believe at first that I pay three forty for an ordinary suit. Showed 'em the tailor's bill, and than convinced 'em. Brand-new suit, only had been cleaned once. Matter of fact, it'd just got back from the cleaner's. It was hanging inside the service entrance. He must have just lifted it on the spur of the moment, when he was on his way out."

"Did you see him?"

"I didn't Mabel did—my wife. Apparently she had quite a long conversation with him. How about that for gullibility—inviting him into our home and treating him like a king while he was stealing her gewgaws right under her nose." He clucked derisively. "Why do you ask? Do you have another suspect for her to look over?"

"I have some pictures here." I tapped my briefcase. "Can I speak to your wife?"

"Don't see why not." He opened his mouth to shout for her and then thought better of it, touching a bell-push in the wall instead. "Might as well get some use out of the servants," he said. "Lord knows they cost me enough. That maid alone gets two hundred a month and her keep. They paid *me* less than that when I started with the company—''

I warded off biography with a question: "Did I understand you to say there was a suspect arrested?"

"They didn't arrest him. He was the wrong man. Mabel may be gullible, but she does have an eye for faces. I'd trust her memory for faces any time. They didn't even bring the police into it. No case."

"Who asked your wife to look at him?"

"The insurance investigator. That was the day after they recovered the wristwatch. I had to pay back the money they gave me for the wristwatch. Two hundred dollars. It wasn't one of her good ones. She keeps the one with the diamonds locked up in the safe."

I hadn't often interviewed a more willing, or a more confusing witness. "So the insurance investigator recovered a wristwatch?" I said hopefully.

"That's right. It turned up a couple of weeks ago in a pawnshop in east Los Angeles. They traced the man that pawned it: he's a photographer out in Pacific Palisades."

"A photographer."

"Yeah. The burglar was a photographer, too, or claimed to be. But it wasn't the same man. The one that pawned the wristwatch said he bought it from a customer. Apparently he was telling the truth, Mabel went out to his place in Pacific Palisades with the insurance man. She walked right into the shop and talked to the fellow, pretended to be interested in getting her picture took. She got a bang out of that, Mabel's still an actress at heart. Mabel was a very great actress at one time. I directed her myself in thirteen pictures."

The maid appeared in the doorway. "You want me, Mr. Richards?"

"Ask Mrs. Richards to come out here—to join me in the library."

I said when the maid had gone: "Is Mrs. Richards in good health? No heart condition or anything like that?"

"Mabel's as strong as a horse." He looked at me inquiringly.

"These pictures I have are pictures of a dead man."

"He's dead?"

"Not only that. He's pretty badly smashed. I thought you should be warned."

"Mabel can take it."

"Take what, Jason?"

A woman had quietly entered the room behind us. She was slender and tall in a black evening-sheath. Her graying brunette head was small and handsome, set off by fine tanned shoulders.

"What can I take? What are you letting me in for now?" She was smiling.

"The officer here—Mr. Cross?—has some pictures of a dead body."

"What on earth for, Mr. Cross?"

"I think it's the man who burglarized your house."

"He didn't exactly *burglarize*—"

"No," Richards said. "You invited him over and practically handed him the stuff on a silver platter. If it wasn't for the insurance, I'd be out fourteen hundred and twenty dollars. No." The adding machine in his head clicked, almost audibly. "Twelve twenty, after they recovered the wristwatch for me."

His wife laid a hand on his arm and regarded him with calm tolerance: "But you *did* have insurance, so you're not out a penny. I admit I was taken in, though."

"How did it happen, Mrs. Richards?"

"Oh, quite naturally. This very pleasant-voiced young man called me up one morning early in February."

"It was January," her husband said. "January the twelfth."

"January, then. He said he was a photographer with some home magazine, and he'd heard about our house, how beautifully done it was, and would I mind if he came and took some pictures. I said certainly not. I'm a notorious sucker, and oh so very house-proud."

"Naturally," her husband said. "You've got a fine big

house, why shouldn't you be proud of it? It cost into six figures. . . ."

"Be quiet, Jason. He turned up later in the morning with his equipment. I showed him over the house, and he took his pictures, or pretended to. It never occurred to me to be suspicious, and I admit I was pretty careless leaving him alone in some of the rooms. Well, to make a long story short, he picked up everything loose and thanked me and bowed himself out. I even gave him a bottle of beer to drink."

"Ale," her husband said. "Bass Ale, imported from the old country."

"At fabulous cost," she said with a laugh. "Don't mind Jason, Mr. Cross. He's not really avaricious. He just expresses his feelings in money terms. How much am I worth, Jason?"

"To me, you mean?"

"To you."

"One million dollars."

"Piker," she said, and pinched his cheek. "Does anybody bid a million one?"

He flushed. "Don't say that. It isn't ladylike."

"I'm not a lady." She turned to me, her smile fading. "I'm ready to see your pictures, Mr. Cross."

I showed them to her, looking from them to her face. She had become very grave.

"Poor man. What happened to him?"

"He was run over. Do you recognize him?"

"I think it's the chap, all right. I couldn't swear to it."

"You're reasonably sure?"

"I think so. When was he killed?"

"Last February."

She handed the pictures back and looked up at her husband. "You see. I told you the man in Pacific Palisades wasn't the one. He is older and darker and heavier, an entirely different type."

"I'd still like to talk to him," I said. "Where is his shop, exactly."

"I don't recall the address. Let me see if I can describe it to you. You know the stoplight where Sunset Boulevard runs into the coast highway? It's half a mile or so north of there, one of those slummy little buildings crowded between the highway and the beach."

"On the left-hand side as you go north?"

"Yes. I don't think you can miss it. It's the only photography studio anywhere along there, and there's some kind of a sign, and photographs in the window. Old *dirty* photographs, colored by hand." She shrugged her bare shoulders as if to shake off an atmosphere. "It was one of the most depressing places I've ever been in."

"Why?"

"It was so obviously a failure—everything was in a mess. The man didn't even know his business."

"Mabel can't stand failure," Richards said. "It reminds her of her early life. My wife had a very rough time as a young girl, before I discovered her."

"Before *I* discovered *you*, Jason."

"Your husband told me you talked to the man."

"I did. The insurance investigator suggested I go in and pose as a customer, in order to have a good look at him, and hear his voice. I made a few inquiries about sizes and prices. He couldn't even answer them without asking the girl."

"What girl?"

"He had a little blonde assisting him, probably his wife. Heaven knows he couldn't be making enough in that shop to pay her a salary. The girl was rather nice, at least my vanity thought so. You see, she recognized me. Apparently she'd been catching some of my old pictures on television—"

"Don't mention that awful word!" her husband cried.

"Sorry. She asked me for my autograph, can you imagine? Nobody's asked for my autograph for ages."

"Can you describe her?"

"She was a rather pretty little thing, with a turned-in page boy bob. I noticed her eyes. She had lovely dark blue eyes, but the general effect was spoiled by her paint job. She wore too much of everything—too much lipstick and powder, even eye-shadow. Now that I think about it, I'm certain she was his wife. I remember she called him Art."

Art Lemp and Molly Fawn. The inside of my mouth went dry. "And the man, Mrs. Richards? What did he look like?"

She sensed my excitement, and answered with great care: "The best word I can find for him is amorphous. He had one of those loose, rubbery mouths—how can I describe it? The sort of mouth that can turn into anything. I pay attention to mouths, they're so important in expressing character—"

"Age?"

"It's hard to tell. About fifty-five or sixty."

"Did he have a bald head?"

"No. I do recall wondering if he was wearing a hair-piece. His hair was too sleek and neat, you know? It didn't go with the rest of him."

I moved towards the hall. "Thank you very much, both of you. You've been extremely helpful."

"I hope so," she said.

Richards followed me to the front door. "What is this all about, Cross? Is he a receiver of stolen goods?"

"The story's a little too long to tell you now. I'm pressed for time."

"Whatever you say." He stepped out onto the porch and filled his lungs with air. "Wonderful night, great view. I like to have the university down there. That cultural atmosphere, it makes me feel good. I'm a bear for culture."

"Physical culture," his wife said from the doorway. "Good night, Mr. Cross. Good luck."

CHAPTER
17

I made a left turn on to Sunset and joined the westward flight of automobiles. I passed a few cars, came up behind a fast Cadillac and let it pace me on the unbanked curves. The depression that had blanketed me all day, ever since I learned the boy was stolen, was lifting at the corners. The boy was as lost as ever, but at least I was doing something about it, moving in a long descending curve towards the heart of the evil.

A straight length of road coincided with a gap in the eastbound traffic. I passed the Cadillac, and held the accelerated speed. Approaching headlights rushed up out of the night like terrible eyes and passed with a grunt and a sigh. I slid down the final slope to the coast highway and turned right when the light changed.

Tall eroded cutbanks rose on the inland side. I drove slowly in the left-hand lane, watching the other side. A miscellaneous line of buildings, multicolored and many-shaped, clung to the rim of the road above the beach. Most of them were beach houses on twelve- or fifteen-foot lots, or one-story rental apartments. There were a few shops selling redwood souvenirs, genuine oil-paintings, handwoven textiles, ceramics: Bohemia on its last legs, driven back to the ultimate seacoast. The heavy gray ocean yawned below.

I saw what I was looking for, a storefront wearing a "Photographer" sign, and slowed to a crawl. A truckhorn blasted the rear of my car. I made a hasty left-turn signal and skilled through a break in the southbound traffic. There was no place to park except the shoulder of the highway, close up against the narrow display window.

The window and the shop behind it were dark. In the light from passing cars, I could see the sample pictures through the smeared plate-glass. They were signed, in a large and flowing hand: "Kerry." The names, the lives, the deaths were drawing together towards an intersection.

At the rear of the shop, which wasn't ten feet deep, a hollow rectangle of light outlined a door. I knocked on the glass front-door. The hollow rectangle filled with sudden light. A young woman entered it, pausing with one hand on the knob. She called across the width of the shop, in a voice that sounded tinny through the glass:

"Art? Is that you, Art?"

I shouted back: "I have a message from him."

She stepped forward through the doorway, her giant shadow plunging ahead of her, her tiny heel-taps following. Her face came close up to the glass, a white blur with black holes for eyes and a black mouth, framed in an aureole of lighted yellow hair. I was aware of the skull behind the flesh.

The black mouth trembled: "If he wants to come back, tell him it's no use."

"I came to tell you that."

"I wouldn't touch Art Lemp with a ten-foot pole, not after what he did." She caught her breath: "You came to tell me what?"

"Let me in, Molly. We have things to talk about."

"I don't know you. Who are you anyway?"

"I saw Art today. He wasn't feeling so well."

"I couldn't care less." She was repeating what Bourke had said about her. "If you're a friend of Art's you can go away. And tell him I said so."

"I can't. He isn't hearing so well."

"Buy him a hearing-aid. Good night. Go away." But her face was pressed against the glass, which flattened and widened her nose. She said in a smaller, frightened voice: "What do you want?"

"Information."

"Go and ask Art, why don't you? He always claims he knows it all, he's got the inside dope on everything, and everybody. Ask him."

"He isn't talking."

The dark eyes widened like expanding doubts. "Did they pick him up?" Her mouth was on the glass. When she drew back a little, it left a mouth-shaped lipstick mark.

"This could go on all night, Molly. Let me in and I'll tell you what you want to know. After you tell me."

"How do I know Art isn't with you?"

"Come out and look."

"Oh, no. You're not going to lure me out of here. Who are you? Are you a cop?"

I steeled for that. "A kind of one. I'm a probation officer."

"I'm not on probation. I never been convicted of any crime."

But she unlocked the door and opened it a crack, reluctantly. I planted a foot in the opening.

"I'm as clean as a whistle," she said.

"When did you last see Art?"

"Not for a couple of weeks. We had a big blow-up a couple of weeks ago. I made him get out."

"Is he your husband?"

"I wouldn't say that. We were . . . business partners. I took him into the business when Kerry ran out on me. Not any more, though, I can promise you that. Not since Art laid his filthy paws on me. I'm *glad* he's sick."

She shivered suddenly and violently. "That's a cold wind. I hate the cold sea-wind. If you want to talk, come in. I'm not doing nothing. I haven't done a thing all winter. I haven't had anybody to talk to since Kerry went away."

The chill racked her again. All she had on was a light sleeveless dress.

"Wait a minute, Molly." I fetched my briefcase from the car.

"What have you got in there?"

"I'll show you, inside."

She opened the door and locked it carefully behind me. The back room was a fair-sized studio with two large windows and a door at the rear. Beyond the closed curtains I could hear the wind and the sea gasping and thumping like weary visitors. On one side of the room the tools of the photographer's trade, tripods and light-stands, were stacked in a shadowy jumble against the wall.

The light came from the other side of the studio, where Molly apparently lived. The floor lamp was draped with stockings and underwear. The open davenport bed was violently rumpled, as if its occupant had been wrestling nightmares. There was a gas burner in one corner beside the deep, stained sink lined with coffee grounds. Trampled newspapers littered the floor. The life these things represented had been coming to pieces.

Yet Molly herself was clean and well-groomed. Her pull-taffy hair was lacquer-smooth, her dress freshly laundered. She had lovely white arms.

She covered them with a brown cloth coat and sat on the edge of the bed pulling the coat tight around her. "I hate the sound of that damned sea. Why I ever came out here in the first place..." Her voice drifted lower: "Back where I came from, the nights were warm in summer. It was really nice there, except when there was a storm."

"Where do you come from, Molly?"

The sadness in her eyes changed to sullenness. "None of your damned business. I'm twenty-one. I never did nothing illegal. You can't touch me."

"I'm interested in your friends. Kerry Snow, Art Lieutenant, Fred Miner."

"Fred who?"

"Fred Miner." I described him.

"I don't know the Miner character. The other two, yes. What have they been up to?"

"It's funny you should ask that, Molly."

"Why? You're a cop, aren't you? You didn't come around for the pleasure of my conversation." She swallowed, and slanted a blue glance up at me. "Have you seen Kerry?" Her voice was soft and shy.

"Not lately. When did he leave you?"

"I don't know, it must have been about three months ago. We were only in this place a month. It didn't surprise me. I knew he'd be going after her sooner or later, he was always talking about her that last month."

"I don't follow you."

"Never mind."

"When did you last see him, Molly?"

"I told you, about three months ago. It was February, early February. It know it was before Valentine's Day, because I kept thinking maybe he'd send me one. He didn't." Her glance came up to my face again like a dark blue light. "Are you his parole officer, by any chance?"

"He doesn't need a parole officer. Kerry is dead."

Her teeth clenched. She spoke between them, gutturally. "You're a liar. Kerry couldn't be dead. He's too young to die."

"He died violently, before Valentine's Day."

"Murdered, you mean?"

"I'm trying to find that out."

"Why come to me?"

"Because you knew him."

"I don't believe you. I don't believe he's dead. You're lying to me, trying to break me down."

I showed her Sam Dressen's photographs. Her listless hands turned them over and let them slide to the floor. Twisting her body sideways, she lay down with her legs dragging over the edge of the couch. Her rigid jaws relaxed and her mouth opened wide. Her eyes were wide. She pressed her face into the rumpled sheet and screamed hoarsely for a long time. Then she pulled the coat over her head.

I replaced the pictures in the briefcase. My hands jerked out of control and tore the last one half across.

Molly was very quiet under the coat. Her legs were drawn up to her breast and her head was pressed to her knees. She looked as if she had never been born, or wished she hadn't.

I touched her shoulder, which moved irregularly with her breathing. "Molly."

"Go away. Leave me alone." Her voice was childishly thin, and muffled by the cloth.

"Were you fond of Kerry?"

"What do you think?"

"I think he was murdered."

She flung the coat to one side and raised herself on her arms. Except for the smudged lipstick around her mouth, her face seemed almost serene. There were no tears on it. She rose on her knees. "Who killed him?"

"Nothing's been proved. He was run down by a car. We couldn't even identify him, until tonight."

"Art Lemp," she said. "He came back with Kerry's Chrysler—"

"Back from where?"

"Wherever it was they went. Kerry didn't tell me. He went off with Art that day and I haven't seen him since." She paused, her gaze turned backward and inward. "I heard them talking about it the night before. Art said he knew where the woman was. He promised to take Kerry to her."

"The same woman you mentioned before?"

"Yeah, the one that sent him up. She fingered him for the feds, got him six years in Portsmouth. Kerry was looking for her ever since he got out."

"When was that?"

"Last summer. I met him last summer."

"What was the woman's name?"

"I don't know. All I know about her is what he told me: that she fingered him and he was going to get back at her."

"Where does she live?"

"I don't know. What does it matter, anyway? Art Lemp

was stringing him along, just using the story to get Kerry off someplace where he could murder him.''

"Do you know that, or just imagine it?"

"I know Art Lemp, he couldn't tell the truth to save his life. He come back here with the car, said Kerry sold it to him because Kerry was going away on a trip, he didn't know where. He knew where.''

"You think he took Kerry off on a wild-goose chase and murdered him?''

"So he could move in on me. He was always nuts about me. Nuts is the word. *I* must of been nuts to let him do it.''

"Why did you?''

"To get back at Kerry, mostly. And I was lonely here by myself, and I didn't know how I was going to pay the rent. A big help Art was, laying around half-soused most of the time.''

"When did you kick him out?''

"A couple of weeks ago. I found out he pawned my watch, that Kerry gave me for a wedding-present. We had a big blow-up that night, and the bastard beat me. That was the first and last time. I said to him: get out or I call the cops. The evidence is on my back. It still is.''

She stood up and began to remove her dress.

I said: "Keep it on. Have you seem Lemp since then?''

"I've *heard* from him plenty of times. He keeps calling me up, begging me to let him come back, or else I should go and see him. Big offers, he makes. Mink coat, a new car, a trip to Honolulu. I told him I'd sooner go with a Gila monster.''

"Do you know where he's staying?''

"Down in Long Beach, at some hotel, least he was when he phoned me on Thursday.''

"What hotel?''

"I think it was the Neptune he said. He was crazy for me to come and see him. I told him I wasn't any masochist.''

CHAPTER
18

We drove south towards Santa Monica. It was past eleven, and traffic was slackening off. The city whose fires shone in the sky to the south and east was slowing down like a giant Catherine wheel, shooting off fewer sparks. The Santa Monica beach front was deserted, except for a few last couples depending on love or car heaters to keep them warm. There was a hard offshore wind, which made my front wheels weave a little, and flying clouds over the sea.

With her face averted from me, Molly gazed at their gray invasion.

"I hate this country," she said. "It isn't human country. I look at the ocean and it drives me cuckoo thinking how wide it is, how deep. It's ten thousand miles across, Kerry told me. Did you know that?"

"I crossed it during the war."

"Kerry did, too. His ship was back and forth across it half a dozen times. I was thinking just a minute ago—I must be going cuckoo like I said—I feel like Kerry went away on another long trip across the ocean, too far to ever come back." She leaned forward with her face against the car window. "It's dark out there. It must be lonely all by yourself out there."

She turned her coat collar up around her ears. The top of her head gleamed like a golden egg in a brown nest. When I followed the highway inland, she turned against the back of the seat and watched the sea through the rear window until it disappeared.

"Where did you come from, Molly?"

"I won't tell you. You'll try to send me back."

"I thought you'd want to go back, after the rough time you've been having."

"I never expected the road to be an easy one." Her voice took on a hard obsessive quality, like a fanatic's quoting scripture. "The road to stardom is never an easy one, even if a girl is gifted with beauty and talent both. Read the movie magazines if you don't believe me."

"You're pretty enough. Do you have talent, too?"

"I'm beautiful," she corrected me. "Some very good judges consider me beautiful. I have classical measurements: thirty-five, twenty-three, thirty-five. Those proportions are classical. And I do have talent. I can act. Do you want me to act something? I know some scenes by heart."

"I wouldn't be able to watch you while I'm driving. What brought you out here in the first place, a beauty contest?"

"I have won beauty contests, back home. That's when the judges said that about my classical proportions. I won the bathing-suit part of the state finals. But I came out here on my own."

"Did you run away?"

"I certainly did not. I had my mother's permission. She gave me the bus-fare, even. My mother is quite wealthy. She owns an extensive chain of beauty parlors."

"Where?"

"You can stop trying to get it out of me. I'm not telling."

"Why not, if your mother knows where you are?"

"She doesn't."

"Why not?"

"She's dead. She died last winter, in a flood."

"What about your father?"

"He's dead, too. The whole family was wiped out in the flood."

"So you inherited the beauty parlors."

She paused. "I would of, only the river swept them away. So you see, it isn't any use trying to send me back. I'm staying here until I get a contract, and I'll get one, you just watch. I have the beauty and the talent both."

"How old are you, Molly?"

"Twenty-one."

"Impossible. If you'd been telling lies for twenty-one years, you'd be better at it."

She didn't take offense, but repeated stubbornly: "I'm twenty-one."

I was tired, and had tried to cover too much ground too quickly. Before she closed up entirely, I changed the subject: "What kind of a ship was Kerry on?"

"Some kind of a carrier, he said. He called it a jeep carrier, he tried to kid me that that mean it carried jeeps, but it was airplanes. He was the ship photographer. That's where he got his start as a photographer, in the Navy."

"Did you know the name of the ship?"

"I did. Let me think. It was something with 'Bay' in it."

"*Eureka Bay*."

"That's it, *Eureka Bay*."

"Fred Miner served on the same ship. He was an aviation mechanic. Didn't Kerry ever mention him?"

"You asked me about him before. I told you I never heard of him. What's so important about this Miner character?"

"His car was the one that ran Kerry down in February."

"You said it was Art Lemp."

"That was your idea. But I still think Lemp had something to do with it."

"I know he did. Art was always jealous of Kerry. He knew me first, and he thought he had a right to me. After we got married—"

"Were you and Kerry really married?"

"Sure we were. I can prove it. Even after that, Art was always sniffing around, trying to get me, trying to talk Kerry into some of his crooked plans. That Art Lemp is a crook. He used to be a cop, and they're the worst. Lilies that fester smell much worse than stinkweeds, I learned that in high school."

"And Kerry wasn't a crook?"

"Kerry was different. He was an artistic personality. That's why Kerry and me matched up so well. Maybe he did a few things wrong in his life. Who hasn't?"

"You said he spent time in Portsmouth."

"Six years of it, but it wasn't Kerry's fault. He got taken advantage of."

"Open up the glove compartment in front of you. There's a camera in there. I want you to look at it."

"A camera? Why?" She did as she was told.

I turned the dash lights up. "Have you ever seen that before?"

"Maybe I have. Where did you get it? I think it's the camera he lost."

"Was it Kerry's camera?"

"He had it."

"What does that mean?"

"I was just going to tell you. He didn't really mean to steal the cameras. He told me all about it. His ship was in the drydock at San Diego, and he met this red-headed woman at a party—"

"What was her name?"

"He never called her by name, he called her the red-headed woman. He told me she infatuated him. She talked him into going over the hill from his ship, then when she tired of him she turned him over to the F.B.I. He had a couple of cameras with him from the ship that he forgot to take back, so they had him for A.W.O.L. and theft of government property and everything. This camera they didn't find, though, he stashed it at a friend's house."

My right foot stamped the accelerator. We were on a stretch of highway that lay level and straight as a causeway across the salt flats. Away to our left and behind us, the lights of the airport flared in a giants' biovuac. A plane rose wobbling through them like a vulture heavy with carrion. Night in these regions had an unredeemed ugliness. I wrestled the steering-wheel while the speedometer turned past eighty, hoping to leave the ugliness behind.

It rode in front of my eyes, a red-haired woman with a naked back.

"Is that your story, or Kerry's?"

"It's the honest truth. Kerry always told me the truth."

"You should try it yourself some time." I couldn't keep the bitterness out of my voice.

That or the speed frightened her. "I did tell the truth, I'm no liar. Where are we going?"

"To see Art Lemp."

"I don't believe you. You're the one that's lying. You're taking me some place, you're going to send me away."

My nerves were pulled wire-thin. "Shut up. Be quiet."

She was suddenly too quite. I looked away from the speeding gray road and saw her fumbling in the lighted glove-compartment. I kept an automatic at the back of it. It came out in her hand.

Instinctively I pressed the brake, too hard. The car rocked and screeched. Molly said: "That's right, stop the car. This is the end of the ride. And you're the one that's getting out." She held the gun two-handed, steadily.

It was a service forty-five, heavy enough to cut me in half. I took my time about stopping the car. I couldn't remember whether the automatic was actuated.

If it was, a slight pressure on the trigger would end me. If it wasn't she couldn't fire the gun. It took a fairly strong man to ready it for firing.

The car ground to a stop on the cinder shoulder. The shallow ditch was paved with empty cans. A sulfur stench fouled the air. On the rim of the plain, against the cloudy reflection of the city, the oil derricks stood like watchtowers around a prison camp where nothing lived.

I had come to the wrong place, at the wrong time, and done the wrong thing. A law officer who let a prisoner take his gun was worse than a fool. I set the emergency brake, my stomach expecting disaster.

"Don't bother with that," she said. "You're getting out, and leave the keys where they are."

"I'm staying in."

"No you're not. I warn you, I'll shoot. You're not sending me back to Minnesota for people to laugh at, or frame me with a camera I never stole. I'll kill you first."

Her eyes were a blind and stormy blue.

"The gun isn't actuated, Molly. It won't fire."

She grasped the barrel-jacket and wrestled with it, pressing with all her might. The muzzle turned downward, away from me. I got one hand on it, and then the other.

She scratched the backs of my hands. I twisted the gun away from her, held it out the window and fired into the wasteland. Its recoil, only half-expected, flung my arm up. I set the safety very carefully and dropped the gun in the left-hand pocket of my jacket.

"It was actuated. You might have killed me. Then what would you have done?"

"You got plenty on me now," she said glumly. "Now you can put me away for a long time."

"I'm not interested in doing that. I'd like to find a place for you where old men won't beat you, where young men won't die on you." After the shot, I had no anger left in me.

"Is there a place like that?"

Her gaze slipped past me, across the black fields, to the tower-ringed horizon. The odor of burning was still strong on the air.

We drove on into Long Beach.

CHAPTER
19

The Neptune Hotel stood in the limbo of side streets between the neons of the business section and the dark waterfront. Its own sign, ROOM WITH BATH, *$1.50,* flickered and went out and came to life again like a palsied lust. Flanking the hotel entrance was a bar where a few sailors and their fewer girls sat with midnight faces. The lobby was dimly lit and unpeopled. Its green-washed walls cast a pallor on Molly's face and turned her blown hair to green gold. She looked around the lobby as if she had been in similar places before.

The night clerk stood up behind his desk. He was a dark young man with an advanced haircut, short on top and long around the ears. He wore a luminescent scarlet shirt and illustrated suspenders.

"You want a double?" he said in a cynical tenor.

"No."

"You take her up to a single, you pay the same as a double."

"I'm a police officer."

He ducked, ran his fingers through his short top-hair, and came up smiling. "Why didn't you say so?"

"You have a man named Arthur Lemp staying here."

He glanced at the brass-hooked key-rack behind him. "Lemp is out."

"When did he leave?"

"I couldn't tell you that. I haven't seen him tonight, or last night either."

"When did you see him?"

"Night before last, I guess. One night is like another." He moved one hand palm-down across the flat surface of his nights.

"Who was he with?"

"I never saw him with nobody. He's a loner."

"No friends?"

"Not that I ever saw. He always come by himself. That's the only time I saw him, when he come in for the night. It was generally pretty late, around this time."

"Where did he spend his evenings?"

He inverted the eloquent hand. "How would I know? The bars. I'm not his cycloanalyst. But he's got the flybar look."

Molly snorted.

"He's traded it in on the mortuary look," I said.

The young man touched his mouth, and then the side of his nose. "Dead?"

I nodded.

Molly's hand gripped my elbow. Her outraged whisper hissed in my ear: "You didn't tell me he was dead. You been conning me. You brought me down here under false pretenses."

I shook off her hand, and spoke to the clerk: "Lemp was murdered this morning, out of town. I want to look at his room."

"You got a warrant?"

"I don't need a warrant. This is a homicide case. The man is dead."

Shrugging his thin shoulders, he took a tagged key from the rack and pushed it across the desk:

"I guess you know what you're doing. It's three seventeen. Okay if I don't go up with you? I got no replacement here. You turn left from the elevator. It's the last one at the back, by the fire escape."

"Thanks." I turned to Molly. "You're coming up with me."

"I don't want to come up."

"I'm not taking a chance on your running around loose and getting into more trouble."

I took her arm and walked her to the elevator. Its protesting machinery lifted us to the third floor. We went to the left, following a series of small red lights to the end of the corridor. Molly's footsteps dragged.

There were human sounds behind the walls and doors, sounds of unquiet slumber, alcoholic laughter, furtive love. I was tired enough to feel the weight of lives pressing from both sides of the narrow hallway. For a nightmare instant I felt infinitely tiny, a detached cell threading the veins of a giant, tormented body.

The key turned loosely in the lock and passed us into the room. A light switch inside the door controlled the ceiling fixture. A pair of forty-watt bulbs blinked weakly on an iron-framed single bed, a corner washbasin, a rickety bureau, a few square yards of worn carpet.

Across the half-blinded single window the fire escape slanted up, a black-iron Jacob's ladder against the roiled light and darkness over the rooftops.

"So this is where he's been staying," Molly said contemptuously. "In this dump, and he was talking mink and convertibles on the phone. He always was a dirty lying old skunk."

"You seem to be able to handle your grief."

"Why not? You didn't see what he did to me. Look at this."

Shedding her coat abruptly, she reached for the zipper in the back of her dress and bared her shoulder blades. Downward from the base of her neck, the white flesh was crisscrossed with blue-black welts turning green and yellow.

"He did it to me with his Mexican belt that night that I broke with him. You know what he said? Why he did it? That he'd do anything for a little affection. He said he was old and loveless, so he beat me."

"I'm sorry."

"So am I sorry, but not for him." She closed the zipper.

"A swell chance I got of landing any modeling assignments as long as those marks are on my back."

"Sit down and be still now, Molly. I have work to do."

She sat in the room's only chair and looked at the wall. A curved decorator's tool had marked the walls and ceiling with myriad small crescents, like hoofprints left by a revolving army of nightmares.

There was no closet, and nothing on the hooks behind the door. The bureau drawers were empty. I went to the bed, which had been freshly made up, and pulled off the sheets. There was nothing under them but the brown stains on the mattress. I raised the mattress and propped it against the wall. Lemp's suitcase was under the bed.

It was made of tan canvas trimmed with brown leather. The leather was scuffed, and the lock had long since been sprung. It contained a paper parcel from a Chinese laundry, which I didn't bother to open, a pint bottle of cheap bourbon wrapped in a moth-eaten coat sweater, a carefully folded brown suit, with a tarnished San Francisco Police Department badge in the inside breast-pocket, a .38 caliber revolver and a box of shells, a packet of licorice throat-lozenges, a heavy jackknife equipped with a fingernail-clipping device, a pair of black-leather boots with razor slits across the toes, half a ham sandwich moldering in wax paper, an empty alligator wallet, a nearly empty bottle labeled Pote-N-Zee the Hormone Elixir, and a pair of small baby-shoes cast in bronze and tied together with a blue ribbon.

There was a layer of books and papers at the bottom. One of the books was entitled "The Real Meaning of Your Dreams"; the cover illustration was a man's head swelling with fantasies. The nature of Lemp's fantasies was indicated by the other books, most of which were under-the-counter paperbacks with sadistic illustrations. On the flyleaf of one of them, someone had written a verse with an indelible pencil:

Molly Molly it'd be jolly
For you and I to have a frolic little girl

You got a beautiful golden curl
Blue eyes like heaven
Take me up to heaven at eleven
I love you little girl.

REFRAIN:—Jolly little girl with the golden curl.

The papers included a letter written by an Assistant District Attorney of San Diego County in 1941, recommending Lemp's employment as a company guard by a San Diego aircraft plant; a sepia snapshot print of a bald-headed young man who might have been Lemp holding a long-dressed baby under a leafless maple tree; and Lemp's birth certificate. He had been born Arthur George Lempke in Pittsburgh, Pa., on June 14, 1892, to Arthur Lempke, laborer, and his wife Trinity, housewife. As if to bracket his life in a single document, Lemp had written in pencil on the dog-eared official envelope containing his birth certificate:

Timetable—post letter Valley Vista Ranch, Ridge-crest Fri. p.m. not too late—Miner take boy to desert before mail (Sat.) delivered 9-9:30 a.m.—train pulls out station 11 a.m.—plane leaves Int. Airport 2:20 p.m.

But Lemp had been taken up to heaven shortly after eleven, and missed the plane. I opened his bottle of bourbon and had a stiff drink. The room, the contents of the suitcase, the remnants of Lemp's sixty years were infinitely dreary. I felt the shuddering lapse of all those years.

"Stealing a dead man's liquor. Pretty low." Molly got up from her chair and took a few tentative steps towards me. "Mister, I could use a slug of that myself."

"You won't get it from me."

"Why not?" She smiled coaxingly.

"I never give liquor to minors or take candy from babies."

She struck a pose, shoulders back, chest out, stomach in. "I'm no baby. I've been drinking regular for several years."

It struck me with sudden harsh clarity, simultaneously with the crude whisky, that I was at the center of the evil maze. It contained a timetable for a kidnapping packed with a sentimental pair of baby boots, an old man writing a vapid love-poem on the flyleaf of a corrupt book, a young girl who had learned to accept corruption. Molly's smile, as blank as the walls, as threadbare as the carpet, had somehow become the meaning of the room.

"You're a babe in the woods," I said. "Cover yourself with leaves."

Memory came into her eyes like dark ink spreading in water. "You say the darnedest things. I used to do that all the time, cover myself with leaves. I used to play in the leaves in the fall when I was a kid. We used to play house."

"Was that before the flood?"

"Yeah, before the flood."

I squatted down and began to repack the suitcase. There was an angry core of heat in my body. It was hard to hate evil without overdoing the hate and becoming evil. It wasn't Molly I hated, or even Lemp. It was the shades of their desires, the frantic waste of their flesh, the ugly zero waiting at the end.

My hands were awkward. Folding the brown suit, they shook the alligator wallet onto the floor.

Molly scrambled for it on hands and knees.

"Give it to me," I said. "It's all evidence."

"But this belongs to Kerry. I gave it to him for his birthday last year. It was his thirtieth birthday, and I was in the chips for once."

"Are you sure it was his?"

Her fingers were exploring its interior. "It's got his initials in it. I had them put on at the leather shop when I bought it."

She showed me the tiny gold initials in one corner: K. S. "I was right. He murdered Kerry and stole his car and his wallet."

"And his girl."

"It isn't true. Kerry was the only one I loved. Except when he got nasty, Art Lemp was more like a father to me, a grandfather. All he wanted to do was look at me. I was always faithful to Kerry in my heart."

I took the wallet from her hand and finished packing the suitcase. She went to the mirror above the washbasin. After studying her reflection for some time, she said to herself, or to no one in particular:

"I forget who I am sometimes. I can't remember who I am sometimes."

She raised the window and looked out across the fire escape. Red and black were tangled in a skein blown over the rooftops. Distant cries and hootings rose from the city, gusts of sound like wind blowing here and there in an iron forest.

CHAPTER
20

The hideous concrete façade of the courthouse, Moorish-arched and Byzantine-turreted, was lovely to my eyes. The lights in the embrasured windows of the sheriff's wing shone like the lights of home. But Molly hung back: she saw the bars on the windows. I had to help her up the steps and through the door.

I deposited her on a bench in the outer office, with Lemp's suitcase beside her. There were three deputies on night duty instead of the usual one. Six eyes converged on Molly, swinging to me reluctantly when I spoke:

"Any word of the Johnson boy?"

"Not yet. Could be they're not telling us everything. Who's the cutie?"

Molly thrust her shoulders back and posed for the deputies' flashbulb admiration.

"A witness I'm bringing in. Is Sam still on duty?"

"In his office. He won't go home."

"Forest?"

"He set up temporary headquarters in the Clerk's rooms," the man at the telephone desk said. "You want to talk to him, I'll see if I can get you a passport and visa. You ever consorted with Democrats?"

"Don't bother."

"That was a joke, son."

"Ho ho."

"What's the matter, Howie, you losing your sense of humor?" He turned to the other deputies. "Mister Cross done hitched his wagon to a star."

I said: "If you want to do something, order me in some food. I haven't eaten for several weeks."

"I leap to do your bidding, master." He swiveled back to the telephone.

"Thanks. Make it ham and eggs and coffee. I'll be in with Sam."

I tossed a dollar across the counter and took the suitcase and Molly down a tile-floored corridor to Sam Dressen's cubicle. Sam was asleep, his gray head resting on his desk like a large granite paperweight. I shook him and he sat up, blinking and smiling:

"Must have dozed off for a minute. That was red-hot tip, Howie, that business card you gave me. We got one corpse identified already."

"Art Lemp?"

The smile sagged disappointedly. "You know, eh? Where you been?"

"To hell and back. This young lady knew Lemp, and the other one was her husband."

I nodded towards Molly. She was making herself small and

flat against the door-frame. I wondered if she recognized the jail smell that sifted down inevitably from the second floor. Or perhaps it was the WANTED circulars that were the only pinups on Sam's walls.

"You wouldn't kid an old man old enough to be your father, Howie?"

"She's his widow, common-law possibly, but his widow. His name was Kerry Snow."

"We were married in Las Vegas," she cried. "On the fifteenth of January. It was legal!"

"I believe you, Molly. Come in and sit down, and tell us all about it."

A session of questioning followed, until my breakfast arrived. Molly gave us no additional information. Either her men had kept her completely in the dark about their illegal activities, or she was afraid of talking herself into jail. She looked afraid, and hungry.

I shared my toast and coffee with her. Sam had eaten at midnight, he said. It was nearly two.

I stood up, feeling the stiffness in the hinges of my knees. "Is Amy Miner still here?"

"She's in the special cell on the third floor. I'll take you up."

"Who's on duty?"

"Stan Marsland."

"I can run the elevator. You've got work to do, Sam. This suitcase belonged to Lemp. It's loaded with grist for your mill."

His lined face expressed a nice balance of anticipation and foreboding. "Fine," he said doubtfully. "What do I do with the girl?"

"Forest will want to talk to her. Perhaps you'd better turn the suitcase over to him, too. They've got their mobile laboratory down here, haven't they?"

"It's in the garage courtyard."

"Good. You can go home then. Why not take Molly with you? She doesn't want to spend the night in jail."

"I'll say I don't."

Sam regarded his dubiously. "I got a wife already."

"That's the point. I haven't." I turned to her. "If Sheriff Sam puts you up in his house, you won't run away?"

"Where would I run away to?"

"Okay, Howie," he said. "You did enough for me lately. One thing you didn't do, though, you didn't bring back my pictures."

"I will. Give me a few minutes more."

The automatic elevator was the only way to reach the jail floors at night. I rode it up. Stan Marsland was waiting at the top of the shaft with his hand on his holster.

"Isn't it kind of late for visiting-hours?"

"Special circumstances, Stan. How often do we have a kidnapping?"

"Often enough to suit me. What's in the briefcase, food? I hope it's food."

"Files and hacksaws."

"Don't mention them there things." The graveyard shift made everybody garrulous. "I was hoping maybe it contained a steak, onion, fried potatoes, and a glass of draft beer. All of which I could use."

"Is Mrs. Miner awake?"

"I wouldn't know. She probably is. They don't sleep so good the first night. You want to see her?"

"Yes."

"Down here?"

"In her cell will do. It will only take a minute."

He led me up a curved iron stair to an iron-railed gallery with a riveted floor. We passed a series of iron-sheathed doors with small wire-reinforced windows. There were shouts and howls and laughter behind one of them.

"Drunk tank," Marsland said. "It's just like fiesta, on a Saturday night. But oh on Sunday morning!"

At the end of the gallery he unlocked a door and turned me over to a sleepy matron. The women's cells were open cages with barred doors. I could smell perfume among the animal and chemical odors. Amy Miner, alone in a corner cell, was standing at the bars as if she had known I was coming.

"Mr. Cross! You've got to get me out of here."

"Quiet, Amy," the matron said soothingly. "You'll disturb the other girls."

"But I've got no right to be here. I've done nothing wrong."

The matron wagged her head in my direction. Her hair was tied back in an old-fashioned bun that looked as hard and shiny as a doorknob. "Amy's been quite a problem, Mr. Cross. Do you think they'll be letting her out in the morning?" She added in a whisper: "I had to take her stockings off, she was talking about putting an end to herself."

"They have to let me out," Amy was saying. "I've done nothing wrong."

"Your husband has, apparently."

"I don't believe that, either."

"Until it's settled, one way of the other, they're going to have to hold you. I don't like it. Nobody likes it. Still, it's got to be done."

I moved up closer to the bars. A wire-netted light burned feebly in the ceiling. Amy's eyes were puffed from crying. The lines in her face had deepened like erosion scars. Her mouth had set bitterly. Her hair straggled in grayish-brown ropes over her temples.

"What have they done to Fred?"

"Nothing's been heard from him."

"They've killed him, haven't they? They've killed him and stolen the boy and locked me up and thrown the key away."

I didn't like the hysterical lilt in her voice. "Calm down now, Amy. Things could be worse. You'll be out of here in a day or two."

Her hands came through the bars. "Do you promise?"

I took her hands. They were as cold as the metal. "I

think I can promise that. You're being held as a witness, partly for your own good. When you've done your job as a witness, you'll go free.

"But I didn't witness anything."

"You must have. You were married to Fred a long time. How long, ten years?"

"Just about. Long enough to know that Fred's no criminal."

"Wives have been mistaken before." I turned to the matron. "Can we have a little more light?"

She strode to a bank of switches and turned the ceiling light up. For the fourth and last time, I brought the posthumous photographs out of the briefcase.

"Did you ever see this man in your's husband's company?" I held a blown-up full-face to the bars.

She made a sound in her throat: "Augh." Her knuckles strained around the bars, and whitened. "Who is he?"

"He served on the *Eureka Bay*. Your husband must have known him. Fred was aboard the ship from the time it was launched."

"Is it the Snow boy? Is that who it is?"

"Yes. Kerry Snow."

"What happened to him?"

"He's the one Fred ran down in February. These pictures were taken after his death."

"He's dead?"

"Your husband killed him. Did they know each other well?"

"I don't think so. I hardly knew him at all. He came to our flat in Dago once or twice. Fred liked to be hospitable to the younger men. But that was way back in forty-five."

"Has Fred been seeing him since then?"

"I don't know."

"What about Arthur Lemp?"

She answered, after a pause: "I never heard of him."

"You're sure?"

"Why should I lie? You told me if I tell what I know, I go free."

"One more question, Mrs. Miner. There's a possibility that Fred took the boy into the desert. Where would he be likely to go in the desert?"

"I couldn't tell you. I'm sorry. Fred always hated the desert, it bothers his sinuses. When Mr. and Mrs. Johnson went to the desert, they always left Fred behind, after the first time."

"Is that what they did in February?"

"Yes. Mrs. Johnson did the driving."

"Speaking of Mrs. Johnson, how well did Fred know her?"

"She was a good friend of his, she always has been."

"Did they see much of each other before Fred went to work for her?"

"Naturally they did. She was in charge of his ward in the Navy hospital. He was laid up with his back there for nearly a year."

"Did they meet outside the hospital?"

"Not that I know of. Fred didn't get out much, except for a few weekends towards the end." She thrust her gray face forward between the bars. "I know what you're hinting at. It isn't true. Fred never messed with any other woman, let alone Mrs. Johnson. What are you trying to get at, anyway?"

I said I didn't know, and asked the matron to let me out of there.

Forest was questioning Molly in Sam Dressen's office. Their voices came low and monotonous through the closed door:

"Can you prove that you were in bed all morning?"

"There wasn't anybody sitting there watching me."

"Sleeping in is hardly an alibi."

"It's no crime."

"Stabbing a man to death with an icepick is."

"I don't even own an icepick."

I knocked on the door and handed Sam his photographs. Neither Forest nor Molly looked at me. They were absorbed in their question-and-answer game.

I had seen and heard enough of the girl for one night. She

was my responsibility, in a sense. In a deeper sense, there was nothing I could do for her. Her life was running swiftly by its own momentum, streaking across the midnight like a falling star.

"Take good care of her, Sam," I said out of a sense of inadequacy. Go and catch a falling star.

"The wife will look after her."

"Tell Forest I'm waiting for him."

Someone had abandoned a local newspaper on the bench at the end of the corridor. It carried no story on the kidnapping or the murder. One of the front-page items interested me, however. My matron had succumbed to her kleptomania once again. Out on bail, she had walked into a department store and stolen two bathing-suits, size nine.

I leaned my head back against the wall and lapsed into a coma, approximating sleep. Forest's quick footsteps aroused me. He sat down on the bench, looking as sharp and well groomed as he had that afternoon, but just a little white around the mouth.

"You've been doing some nice work, Cross. I had my doubts about your wild-goosing off by yourself, but you seem to have an instinct."

"I know the local people. That always helps. Sam Dressen there, for example, is getting a little old and slow, but he'll die trying."

"I told him to get some rest. How did you happen to turn up the girl?"

"That story can wait. You talked to Bourke?"

"I did. What's your opinion of him?"

"A sharp operator, but cautious."

"You don't think he could be the mastermind behind all this?"

"Not Bourke. He was too ready with his information, and it checked. I think Arthur Lemp plotted the kidnapping himself." From my inside pocket, I produced the penciled envelope containing Lemp's birth certificate. "This seems to be proof of it."

Forest read the "timetable" aloud, punctuating the reading with an exclamatory whistle. "Miner's definitely in it then. What's this about taking the boy to the desert?"

"I can't add anything to that. There's a lot of desert in California."

Forest thought in silence for a minute, biting the inside of his upper lip. "Lemp plotted the kidnapping, it would seem He didn't plot his own murder."

"That seems to be a reasonable working-hypothesis."

Forest smiled, rather grimly. "And it isn't likely that Miner killed him. His assignment was to dispose of the boy. Certainly he'd get out of town before the ransom letter was delivered. A third member of the gang is indicated."

"Or nonmember. Lemp was a very small-time criminal, until today. A big-time criminal, or an organized mob, may have got wind of his plan and decided to pluck the reward."

Forest said, musingly: "Murder Incorporated favored the icepick m.o. But then, a number of private individuals have, too. Icepicks are too convenient. What do you think of the Fawn girl as a possibility? She was in a position, or could have been, to know what was going on."

"It's possible she did it. Not very probable, though. If she had fifty thousand dollars cached somewhere, she wouldn't sit around and wait to be picked up."

"If she was smart."

"She isn't. In her world, everyone's either a victim or a victimizer. She's a victim."

"Worms can turn, littler fleas have littler fleas, and all that. She had reason to hate this Lemp, I understand, which gives her a double motive."

"Frankly, I'm more interested in her husband—her ex-husband, Kerry Snow. I've established a connection between him and Miner. They served on the same Navy vessel during the war, and Snow and Miner were friendly acquaintances. I got that out of Mrs. Miner just now. So long as there was no connection, Miner could claim it was a hit-run accident. Not any more."

"I had a feeling," Forest said. "What ship were they one?"

"The *Eureka Bay*. Kerry Snow was ship's photographer."

"Damn my eyes!" He struck himself sharply on the scalp with his clenched fist, but in such a way as not to disturb the part. "I should have remembered that name of that ship from your report on Miner. We've got a record on Snow, you see. As soon as we ascertained his name, I teletyped Washington. Our Los Angeles office arrested him in January 1946. We turned him over to the Naval authorities as a deserter. They found him guilty on a desertion charge, and another charge of theft of Navy property. He served six years and four months in Portsmouth, and was released last spring."

"Molly told me some of that."

"Do you know who gave us the information that led to his arrest in 1946?"

"She mentioned a red-headed woman—"

"No, sir. Snow's Los Angeles address was provided to us by Lieutenant (j.g.) Lawrence Seifel, then attached to the Eleventh Naval District in San Diego."

"Are you certain?"

"There's no mistake. His name is on file in the Los Angeles office. We keep fairly thorough records on our cases," he said a little combatively. "What do you know about Seifel?"

"Not too much. He seems to be very intelligent, and very nervous. I should say, for the record, you haven't seen him at his best today, he's having private troubles of some kind. You did see him?"

"Naturally, as soon as his name turned up."

"A mutual acquaintance says he's money-hungry and highly egotistical. And Seifel did know Lemp slightly, by his own admission."

"Lemp approached him, once, according to his story. As for the Kerry Snow affair, he admits he must have given us the address of Snow's hideout, since it's on the record, but he claims he doesn't recall the circumstances, or even the name. His wartime job was handling courts-martial for the Eleventh Naval District, and as he says scores of cases passed through his hands. So it's possible he's telling the truth, and actually doesn't remember.''

"Where is he now? At home?''

"When he left here, about eleven, he was going out to the Johnson place. He said he wanted to do whatever he could for Mrs. Johnson in her bereavement.'' Forest's tone was edged with sardonic mimicry.

"Bereavement! Is the boy dead?''

"Johnson is. I thought you'd have heard about it.''

"Has he been murdered, too?''

"He died a natural death, early this morning. I suppose you could call it indirect murder. The doctor told me the strain was too much for his heart.''

CHAPTER
21

I drove up to the summit of the ridge. The night was still and silent, balanced on its dead center. The city's web of lights lay behind me like a tangled net hauled phosphorescent from the sea and flung up along the slopes. Beyond, the sea itself was a gray emptiness lit between the moving clouds by a few small hurrying stars.

In the hedged tunnel of road where Kerry Snow had met his death, the darkness beyond my headlights was so solid that day was unimaginable. Murder was imaginable, though. I could see the three of them: the faceless victim fallen in the road, the blind-drunk murderer driving on over him, and

Arthur Lemp watching from the darkness, planning to fashion a second crime from the leavings of the first.

I shifted into second and let the motor's inertia hold the car on the descending curves. My own excitement had long since settled down into a stubborn anger. If the boy was alive, I was determined to find him. If the boy was dead, his death would have to be paid for.

My headlights swept the gatehouse where Miner had lived, where Miner would live no longer. In the drive ahead, long brown leaves from the eucalyptus trees formed desolate hieroglyphics on the stones. The trees themselves stood overhead like tremulous giants, shaking in fear of the wind and the shifting sky.

There was a car in the turnaround, and lights from the main house spilled down into the ravine. The car was a new Buick convertible, which I associated with Larry Seifel.

Seifel answered the door. His eyes looked sleepy, and a little out of focus. Passing him in the doorway, I caught a whiff of his breath, pungent with alcohol. He stopped me in the glass-bricked entrance hall and spoke for the first time, in a whisper.

"You know what's happened, don't you?"

"A lot of things have happened."

His hand grew heavier on my arm. "I mean the old man. He died tonight—last night."

"Forest just told me. Are they going to have an autopsy?"

"I don't see why they should. The doctor assured Helen it was the coronary, nothing else."

"That must have been a great comfort to her."

His mouth opened, unevenly. "Does that have some hidden meaning?"

"The things that have been happening have," I said. "I'm trying to find it. Now here's a possibility that should be interesting to the legal mind. A man is seriously ill. It's known that excessive excitement is likely to kill him. A highly exciting event is made to occur; a kidnapping, to be exact. The man dies, and the question is: Is it murder?"

"Are you asking me for my opinion? I'd say its arguable. There have been comparable cases where murder has been proved—"

"I'm asking you for your evidence. Forest tells me you turned in Kerry Snow for desertion in 1946. I don't believe you could have done that to a man and not remember it."

"Are you calling me a liar?"

"I'm suggesting that the memory is a voluntary faculty, to a great extent. It can be turned off and on. You should get to work on yours."

"I've taken enough from you today. Who do you think you are?"

"Diogenes. I have a Diogenes complex. What's yours?"

"Œdipus," Helen Johnson said from the inner doorway. "Larry's as Œdipal as all get out. We were just discussing it before you arrived. Abel was Larry's father-image, he says. Now that his father-image is kaput, Larry has an irresistible urge to possess the father-image's wife-image. That is, me. Isn't that what you said, Larry?"

"You're a fast worker, Seifel."

"Go to hell." His mouth twisted sideways. His hand on my arm jerked me around towards him. His right fist rose rapidly towards my face.

I parried the uppercut with my left forearm, stepped in close and locked his arms in a bear-hug. "When are you going to grow up? A punch in the nose never helped any situation."

I knew Seifel's type, had been dealing with it most of my adult life: the anxious ego walling itself in behind an adipose tissue of bluff and vanity.

"Turn my arms loose. I'll show you who's grown up, I'll knock your block off." He struggled to free himself, tears of anger rising in his eyes. Humiliation in front of a woman was hard for him to bear. No doubt he had had enough of it from his mother.

Helen Johnson came forward and put a hand on his shoulder: "Calm down now, Larry. If you don't I'm going to have to ask you to leave."

He became perfectly still at her touch, though the tension stayed in his muscles. I released him. He turned to her in a trembling rage:

"You didn't hear what he said."

"What didn't I hear?" She was very calm, perhaps too calm. Her beauty had grown colder with the night, colder and darker. There were lines in her brow, smudges of doubt in her eyes, distinct blue semicircles under them.

"He virtually accused you of murdering your husband. He definitely accused me of withholding information."

"Well?" she said to me with a slight unchanging smile.

"Mr. Seifel is exaggerating. Forest, the F.B.I. man, referred to your husband's death as indirect murder. I asked Mr. Seifel for a lawyer's opinion: whether or not the kidnappers are legally responsible for your husband's death."

"Where did I come in?"

"You didn't, until now."

"Is that why you came out here at this hour—to ask Larry for a legal opinion?"

"There are several things I'd like to go into."

"Let's stick to the subject of Abel's death. I've been thinking about it all evening—all night. I think I had better tell you the truth about it. There's something about the truth—"

Seifel moved slightly, placing one dinner-jacketed shoulder in front of one of her shoulders. "Don't say another word, Helen. You're foolish to commit yourself on anything when you're in an emotional state."

She didn't look at him. "As I was saying, in my emotional way, the truth has a saving grace. It's something to hold on to when you're falling through space—you know?—even when it's bitter. Besides, I feel I owe it to myself, in my capacity as non-grief-stricken widow."

Her brittleness was disquieting. I said: "Can we go in and sit down?"

"Of course. Forgive me. You must be exhausted. Mr.

Forest gave me some idea of what you were trying to do. I can't tell you how grateful—"

"For nothing," I said. "Until you get Jamie back, it adds up to nothing."

"No, I don't agree." There were sudden tears in her eyes. "But do come in."

She seated me on a sectional divan that curved around the fireplace in a corner of the living-room. Eucalyptus logs were burning low in the grate, giving off a faintly medicinal odor. The indirect lights were dim along the walls, and night pressed heavily on the great window.

"What will you drink, Mr. Cross? Larry will be glad to make you a drink, won't you Larry?"

"Of course," he answered in a low disgruntled tone.

"You're very kind, but I'm afraid I can't. It might knock me out at this late stage."

"Have one yourself then, Larry," she said. "You know where the liquor is."

He wandered out. She sat above me, on the square back of the divan:

"I used to like Larry. Lately he's been getting on my nerves. Tonight was the last straw. He had the infernal gall to propose to me. He thought that now was the time for us to run away together and live happily ever after. Can you imagine, under these circumstances?"

"Yes. I can imagine."

"I was on the point of ordering him out of the house."

"Why didn't you?"

"I was afraid to be left alone."

"No friends or relatives?"

"None that I've wanted to be with. I wired my mother in New York and she'll probably fly out tomorrow or the next day." She lowered her voice. "Larry's been quite a disappointment to me. I thought I could trust him to be tactful at least."

"He's been drinking since afternoon. It's one way to lose one's inhibitions."

"The problem is to have inhibitions, isn't it? So many people don't have any at all any more. They do as they please, and more often than not it pleases them to ruin their own lives." Her head, half bowed over me, was like a brooding queen's. "What sort of a man are you, Mr. Cross?"

"You don't expect an honest answer."

"Yes."

"I'm a slightly displaced person, I think. Nothing quite suits me, or rather I don't quite suit."

"Is that why you've never married?"

I leaned forward and struck the dying logs with a poker. A swarm of sparks rose like angry hornets and trailed up the chimney. I stood up facing her across the divan.

"You and Ann Devon have been talking about me."

"Why not?"

"Did you talk about Larry Seifel?"

"Naturally. She's very much in love with him, and I think Larry's fond of her if he'll admit it to himself. But you're evading my question."

"You asked for an honest answer. I had none. The question never came up. I suppose the answer to it is something like this: It's part of my displacement. I feel more strongly for other people than I do for myself. For one thing, my parents had a bad marriage. It seems to me I spent a lot of my time when I was a kid trying to head off quarrels, or dampen down quarrels that had already started. Then I started college in the depths of the Depression. I majored in sociology. I wanted to help people. Helpfulness was like a religion with a lot of us in those days. It's only in the last few years, since the war, that I've started to see around it. I see that helping other people can be an evasion of oneself, and the source of a good deal of smug self-satisfaction. But it takes the emotions a long time to catch up. I'm emotionally rather backward."

"Do you honestly believe that?" Her eyes were dark and glowing.

I didn't answer because I had no answer. Nobody knows himself, until later. I shrugged my shoulders.

"I understand what you mean about helpfulness. Every good nurse has a broad streak of it. I've always prided myself on it. Isn't it a virtue?"

"Most human qualities are, when they're not in excess."

"But how could—how could a desire to help someone else be wrong?"

"You have to judge things by their consequences." I looked around for Seifel, and saw that he was nowhere insight. I decided to strike boldly: "I don't know why you married Abel Johnson. If you married him for any reason but love, you shouldn't have."

"What right have you to say that?"

"None. But it hasn't worked out."

The flickering fire cast her shadow high up the wall. It wavered there like a woman clothed in black flames.

"I loved him," she said, "in a way. Naturally I knew he was rich, and I'd worked hard all my life, but that isn't why I married him."

"What way?"

"You're being cruel," she said with her face averted.

"Events are being cruel. I want to see them end."

"I pitied Abel. He begged me to be his wife, to look after him. He was lonely, and afraid of dying. And he wanted a son so badly. . . . You were right, though. I admit it. It didn't work out."

"Why not?"

"He was so much older. I was a strain on him. He tried so hard to keep up. Even Jamie was hard on him. Abel was like a grandfather to the child. He loved him, but he couldn't stand him under his feet all day. That's one reason I let Jamie spend so much time with Fred Miner. It was my worst mistake. I made so many mistakes."

She wrung her hands. They were so dry that I could hear their friction.

"Your husband made mistakes, too. You mustn't blame yourself entirely."

She gave me a startled look. "Yes, I was going to tell you. I find I haven't the heart. But perhaps you know?"

"I've talked with a man named Bourke, who runs a detective agency in Hollywood."

Her hands went to her bosom, and she sighed. Like a frozen flame, dark fire converted into substance, her hair curved over her forehead. It seemed to me that, guilty or not, she was a magnificent woman.

"I was faithful to Abel," she said. "It's strange that I should be telling you this. I've never discussed it with anyone, I don't expect I ever will again. I was genuinely innocent. Perhaps I was indiscreet in letting Larry take me places. I didn't know until today that Abel was suspicious of me, at least to that extent. Of course I knew he was jealous."

"Any man would be."

"Any *old* man, perhaps. You see, I haven't much pity for him now. It seeped out of me gradually. The last drop of it went today, when he told me what he had done. To put a spy on me!" she said. "When all I've thought about in the last six years was looking after him."

"He told you that he had?"

"Yes, he did. When I came home from the mortuary, I described the dead man to him. I thought he might have seen him at the station. Abel recognized the description, but not from the station. It was a private detective he'd put on my trail some time last fall."

She rose and went to the window, her shadow looming across the wall like a dark fate, the one who did the cutting:

"He realized what he had done. It was Abel himself who brought that dead man into our lives in the first place. He made that false move against me, and everything else followed from it." She paused. "Did you really accuse me of murdering Abel, as Larry said?"

"Larry was jumping to conclusions. I admit the possibility occurred to me."

"Well, I didn't. Abel killed himself. He couldn't live with the thought of what he had done. He told me that some time before he died."

"He committed suicide?"

"I don't like to call it by that name. He didn't shoot himself, or take poison. It wasn't necessary, in his condition. Abel got up out of bed and destroyed the furniture in his room. He broke it up, piece by piece, with his hands. I tried to stop him, but it was no use. He threatened to kill me if I set foot in there. He died of the effort, and the anger with himself. When things were quiet and I dared to go in, I found him in the wreckage."

"Why don't you try for some rest now, Helen? You've had a terrible day."

"I can't. I've had an incredible day, but I can't even think about sleep."

"I have some Nembutals at home."

"No," she answered brusquely. "I have pills, too. I prefer not to sleep. I know it's irrational but I have the feeling that if I keep thinking I'll be able to think where Jamie is."

"You love him, don't you?"

"Everybody does. I love him most. He's my son."

"The chances are Miner is holding him somewhere in the desert." I told her about Lemp's "timetable," which I had given to Forest. "Do you know of any place in the desert where Miner would be likely to take him?"

"No. Fred always hated the desert." She added thoughtfully: "We have a cabin in the desert. He wouldn't dare to take Jamie to our own house."

"It's worth considering. It might have struck them as good tactics, on the least-likely principle. Is there anybody in your desert house?"

"Not now. We closed it last month for the season. It's too hot in the summer."

"Where are the keys?"

"Abel kept them in his desk. I'll get them."

She left the room, and returned quickly, looking distraught. "They're gone."

"Where is this place? Does it have a telephone?"

"Of course."

She brought me a telephone and gave me a Palmdale number. At three o'clock in the morning, the call went through immediately. Among husky rumors of transcontinental conversations, I heard the rural telephone ring four times, then four more times. The receiver at the other end was lifted.

"Pacific Point calling," the operator said.

There was a long pause.

"Is anyone there?" the operator said. "Pacific *Point* is *calling*."

The receiver was replaced. There was a colloquy of operators; then: "I'm sorry, sir, your party does not answer."

"But there was someone there?"

"I think so, sir. Shall I have them ring again?"

Close to my ear, Helen cried: "Yes! Please! I *know* he's there. It couldn't be anyone else."

"No, thank you," I said to the operator, and hung up.

Helen grasped my shoulder with both hands, and shook me: "He's there! Talk to him. I have to know."

"No, we might frighten him off. It's possible we've done that already."

Her emotions were swaying in great surges. She cried with equal passion: "Yes! You're right. We've got to go there, now, immediately."

"We?"

"I wouldn't trust anyone else."

I reached for the telephone. "I'll notify Forest."

Her hand closed over mine, slender and strong. "You'll tell no one. I'm taking no chances, understand. Fred Miner can go Scot free if he gives me Jamie back. He can keep the money—"

"How far is it?"

"About a two-hour drive. We can do it faster if we take the Lincoln."

"The F.B.I. can do it still faster by plane."

"I don't care. I want my boy to be alive when we reach him." She was obdurate, her mind completely fixed on one final hope. I made no further attempt to argue with her. She was perfectly ready to go alone if she had to.

"Where's Seifel?" I said. "He might be some use if we run into trouble."

"He went into the pantry to make himself a drink. He never did come out. Hurry and find him."

The lights were on in the butler's pantry, and Seifel had left spoor: a silver pail half-full of melting ice, an icepick floating half-submerged in it, a bottle of Bushmill's Irish Whiskey standing open, a wet ring whitening on the black oak sideboard. Animal noises reached me from another part of the house.

I found him in a bathroom, dousing his head in a basin of cold water. The fluorescent light thrust a white shaft through an open door across the master bedroom, making a cross-section of the chaos Helen had described. In his last hour Abel Johnson had gone berserk. The bed had been dismantled, its coverings torn, the drapes dragged down from the windows, the windows and mirrors smashed. The angry man had fought himself to a finish, bringing his life down in ruins around his own head.

Seifel raised his dripping face and reached for a towel. 'Don't mind me, I've been sick. Feeling much better now. I should never mix my drinks." He shuddered behind the towel.

Above the square blue bathtub in one corner of the room, an Aubrey Beardsley drawing was recessed in the wall behind glass. It depicted a young woman with a swan neck, serpent eyes, hair like a tropical forest. She was perfectly drawn, debonair and evil.

"On your horse," I said to Seifel, who was retying his tie. "We're going for ride."

"A ride? Where to?"

"I'll tell you on the way. Come on. You don't have to look pretty."

"One moment. There's something I wanted to say to you in private."

I was prepared for a fist-fight on the spot, under the eyes of Beardsley's dark-haired lady. But Seifel was truly unpredictable. He said:

"I want to apologize. I'd had too much to drink, and Helen had been rather rough on me. What's more, you were right. I remember Kerry Snow—the name at least; I never saw the man. I turned him in for desertion in '46."

"Without every seeing him?"

"Right. I told the F.B.I. where to find him."

"Where did you get the information?"

He hesitated, swallowing shame. "I have to tell someone, I guess. It might as well be you. Helen gave me the man's address. She asked me to have him apprehended. Just don't tell her I told you." He smiled dismally.

His mechanism seemed obvious. Helen had turned him down, and he was retaliating. An urge to hit him rushed up into my head and almost blinded me. It ebbed like a wave leaving me chilly. Yet I didn't doubt the truth of what he had said.

I thrust it out of the foreground of my thoughts and went outside, with Seifel at my heels. The wind has risen higher. Above the sighing trees the whole sky seemed to be swaying, threatening to topple.

The black Lincoln that had killed Kerry Snow was purring in the drive. Helen was at the wheel. She moved over to let me take it, and explained to Larry Seifel where we were going.

CHAPTER
22

The big car was clumsy on the hillside. I drove in angrily, punishing the brakes and tires on the hairpin curves. The wind died down as we descended. The road uncoiled in a long curve that joined with a two-lane black-top. This ran ruler-straight to the middle of the inland valley, where it met the north-south highway. I pushed the car to ninety and held it there.

Seifel was in the back seat, hunched forward close to my shoulder, watching the road dart backward through the narrow gantlet of the orange groves. Helen held her shot-gun in her lap. No one spoke.

Before we reached Pasadena and the foothills of the mountains, dawn had begun to outline their crags and peaks with an etching-tool. We ascended through fading night into gray day. In the summit of the pass, I switched off the headlights. The sky was a dull green, like stagnant water. Every wrinkle of the cliffs was distinct. Great patches of dirty snow lay at their bases, and along the sides of the road. Their chill edged the wind.

Helen shivered, and drew her leopard-skin coat closer around her shoulders. The gun rolled off her knees and rattled on the floor.

"Be careful with that," I said sharply.

"I am being careful." She retrieved it from the floor.

"Keep it out of sight when we get there. I have a gun in

my pocket, but I'm not planning to use it if I can help it. This is a situation where violence might backfire."

She didn't answer. I glanced at her face, and saw how pale she was. Her eyes, dull and heavy like a reflection of the sky, were gazing far ahead and down across the desert. Its whitish earth, scrawled with winding dirt roads and drifts of brush, stippled with Joshua trees, lay perfectly distinct a mile below. Twenty miles of mountain driving brought us down to it, and into its dust.

I slowed for a crossroads ahead.

"We turn left here," she said. "It's only another five miles. . . . God, how I despise this place, this unholy, empty place. It was never meant for human beings at all. It's the abomination of desolation."

"I understood you came here for winter vacations."

"We did. Abel always had. I couldn't deny him his pleasure. He loved it here, it took him back to his deer-hunting days."

"Fred Miner couldn't take it, is that right?"

"That's true, the dry air bothered him. It's strange he should have chosen this place, under our very noses in a sense, and yet it's the back of beyond. What was it you said at the house, that he was operating on the least-likely principle?"

"We all should have thought of it before. You've read Poe's 'Purloined Letter.' "

"A long time ago, when I was in school."

"Was that so terribly long ago?"

"Æons and æons." She murmured softly and ruefully, to herself: "The purloined boy." Her hands were gripping the stock and barrel of the shotgun.

Marked by a row of country mailboxes, a side road meandered off to the right. One of the mailboxes was stenciled with the name ABEL JOHNSON. Helen touched my arm: "Turn here."

I turned. At the top of the rise, she cried: "Look, you can see the cabin."

I caught a glimpse of the building, a low-roofed stone structure hugging the flat top of a knoll, perhaps a mile away. Straight up from its squat stone chimney, a narrow blue ribbon of smoke was being unreeled onto a transparent green-glass sky. The air was so clear that I could see the light-gray mortar between the moss-dark chimney-stones.

We went down into a shallow arroyo, losing sight of the cabin like a ship in the trough of the waves. The road followed the arroyo bed for half a mile, then climbed the other side. At the top of this second rise, the incredible happened:

"I see him," Helen said. "I see my boy. He's safe."

Seifel leaned forward between us across the back of the seat. "Where is he?"

"See him? He's playing ball. He's all right, Larry. Look."

The boy was on a concrete terrace at the front of the cabin, tossing a rubber ball against the door and trying unsuccessfully to catch it. His red head flared like a tiny beacon.

"Hurry," his mother said beside me. She flung her body forward urgently, as if her movement could increase the speed of the car.

The gun fell across my right foot on the accelerator. I snatched it up and handed it back to Seifel. Helen was oblivious, fixed on the figure of the boy, which appeared and disappeared and appeared again.

At last he saw the Lincoln and recognized it. With a joyful yelp, he dropped his ball and came running out to the road. I braked, but not quickly enough. His mother staggered out of the moving car and fell on her knees in the dust. Then the boy was in her arms.

The door of the cabin opened outward suddenly. Fred Miner came out in his shirtsleeves, an automatic in his hand.

"Mrs. Johnson!" he called on a loud note of surprise. "Is everything okay?"

Almost simultaneously, the shotgun roared from the back seat. One of Miner's arms moved as if it had been pushed backward by an invisible hand. The automatic clanked on the terrace. Miner ran inside.

I turned on Seifel: "Don't be a fool. You'll draw his fire."

"I winged him," he said excitedly.

The boy disengaged himself from the leopard-skin arms. "Why are they shooting at Fred, Mummy? Did he do something wrong?"

"It's only a game, Jamie."

I swung the door wide. "Get into the car, both of you. We're all getting out of here."

But Miner had anticipated us. There was a rapid burst of explosions. The bronze Jaguar shot out of the carport beside the cabin. The top was down, and I could see Miner's face intent over the wheel. The sports car crossed the road in front of us in a flurry of dust, skidded into a turn at the foot of the slope, and turned back to the road a hundred yards behind us. Before I could get the Lincoln turned and straightened out, the Jaguar was a mile or more away, an invisible comet with a winding tail of dust.

I turned to the boy. "Is anybody else out there?"

"No, sir. Just me and Fred."

"Did he treat you all right?"

He looked puzzled.

"He didn't hurt you, Jamie?" his mother said.

"Fred wouldn't—hurt *me*. Fred and me are shipmates."

I said to Seifel: "You stay here with Helen and the boy. Call the police, *et cetera*."

"Let *me* go after him." His face was shining with a kind of buck fever.

"No."

Helen climbed out of the car with the boy in her arms, struggling, and Seifel followed them. I followed Miner's dust.

It was still very early, and there were no other cars. The trail of dust hung in the still air over the road like a curling white worm. It led south across the arid valley, back towards the wall of mountains. Their snow-capped peaks were dazzling now in the full sun.

Twice I caught sight of the Jaguar bouncing over the top of a rise like a low-slung brown rabbit. It was far ahead, and increasing its lead. Since the Lincoln did better than ninety in the straightaways, Miner's car must have been doing well over a hundred. It struck me wryly that he was breaking the conditions of his probation.

I caught sight of it for the third time when it reached the southern rim of the valley, by now a tiny bronze beetle blowing a small derisive spume of dust. It raced below the leaning basalt slabs that buttressed the base of the mountain. Then it was lost in the trees on the shaggy mountainside.

Four minutes and five miles later I was at the foot of the basalt cliffs. Beyond them the road turned sharply and steeply upward. For a screeching, sliding instant the big car threatened to roll. I stamped the gas pedal to the floorboard, braking with my left foot. The rear wheels churned the gravel of the shoulder and pushed back onto the road. Miner's dust was there ahead, obscuring the road and calcuming my windshield.

The desert flora gave way to scrub oaks and these in turn to larger trees, great pines and spruce. The road grew narrower and more treacherous, doubling and redoubling on itself. Far up ahead a patch of snow glittered like a medal on the mountain's shoulder. The road curved around the end of an oval lake that mirrored trees and sky. The higher it went the narrower it grew. I began to hope that Miner, with all his speed, was in a dead end.

Then I saw a gleam of chrome through the trees, and heard him coming. There were no side roads above the lake. The single road we were on was just wide enough for two cars to pass each other. On my left the bank slope up at an angle of forty-five or fifty degrees. On the other side the shoulder fell off sharply into a ravine where a mountain brook rushed downward from the snowbeds.

The Jaguar appeared around a curve, headed directly for me. Miner had come to the end of the road and turned back. I braked and jerked the steering-wheel to the right, skidding to a stop broadside across the road. He didn't slacken speed. If anything, he accelerated. I flung myself backward across the width of the car and fumbled for the door button. But there was no impact.

The Jaguar swerved sharply to my left and climbed the bank. For a moment it looked as if the maneuver might work. Miner was poised above me, forty feet off the road, like a pilot in an open cockpit. Then one of his tires went out with a gunshot report. The Jaguar left the slope, turned turtle in the air, hung there for a long instant with Miner suspended head-down from the steering-wheel, and fell back to earth. Over and over it rolled, down into the road behind me.

Miner was flung out halfway down the slope. He was sitting up when I reached him, coughing bright blood and holding his chest together with one arm. His other arm hung loose, its sleeve soaked with blood. His brow was deeply ridged as if by a giant nutcracker.

His eyes saw me. "Mess. I could of held it with two good arms. Teach me to break the speed laws."

"Why did you do it, Fred?"

"She told me to." His voice was guttural, his breath beginning to bubble. "I know I broke my conditions. But it's pretty rough when you fire on a guy for that."

"It wasn't for that."

"What then? I was only protecting the boy. I brought him out here for his own protection."

"Who told you to do that?"

"Mrs. Johnson. She's the boss."

Then his eyes lost their light, and he toppled. I caught him under his arms. His body was heavier than lead.

CHAPTER
23

I took him back to the desert house, driving slowly because I distrusted my nerves. The wrecked sports car had blocked the road until I had it removed. I finally found a telephone at the ski lift where the road ended, and got in touch with a tow service in Palmdale, forty miles away. It took over two hours altogether. It was midmorning when I reached the Johnson place.

A black custom-built Ford was nosed under the carport. I parked behind it. When I stepped out of the car, the weight of the sun was palpable on my head. The landscape shimmered slightly like a painted curtain concealing a still more desolate reality.

Forest was standing in the doorway with a tall glass of something in his left hand and a revolver in his right hand. He returned the gun to its shoulder holster. "Catch him?"

"He's in the trunk of the car, wrapped in a blanket."

His broad face was impassive. "You had to shoot him, eh?"

"No. He cracked up, trying to get away. Where's Mrs. Johnson?"

"I sent her back home with the boy. She's been singing your praises, incidentally."

My knees softened, threatening to let me down onto the concrete terrace. I turned and braced my back against the stone wall. The shimmering plain divided like curtains blown by a wind, and I saw the more desolate reality behind them: the mask of a woman's face reflected in murky green water.

Seeing that I was in trouble, Forest pushed through the screen door and lent me his shoulder. "Come in, Cross. You've had a rugged twenty-four hours. What you need is a rest and a nice cold drink. Mrs. Johnson made iced tea before she left."

We descended into a room with a low, beamed ceiling and heavily curtained windows. After the outside dazzle, it seemed as dark as a cave. I sat in a creaking cowhide chair. Forest introduced me to a colleague whose name I didn't hear. We agreed that it was hot outside, but comparatively cool inside on account of the thick walls and the cooling system. Forest busied himself in another room and came back with a drink for me. When I had drunk it, I was able to distinguish between the sound of the air-conditioner and the whirring sounds in my head.

Forest gave my shoulder a friendly tap. "Feeling better now?"

"Much better. Thanks."

"This heat is hard on a man when you're not used to it."

"It's cool enough in here," his colleague insisted.

Forest turned to him. "That reminds me, Eddie, we better call Pacific Point and ask them to send a hearse. Cross has Miner's body in the trunk of his car."

"We means me, as usual?"

"What do you think? The telephone's in the kitchen."

Eddie went out. Forest sat down opposite me on a Navajo-blanketed couch. "Miner died without talking, I suppose?"

"He said a little. His head was injured and he may have been irrational. He seemed to think I wanted him for violating probation."

Forest began to laugh, but stopped when I didn't join in. "Is that all he said?"

"He claimed that he was protecting the boy."

"That's what he told the boy." A trace of Forest's

derisive laughter persisted in his voice. "He told the youngster he brought him out her for safety's sake. Is that what he said to you, that the whole thing was done on Mrs. Johnson's orders?"

"Yes, and I got the impression that he was sincere. When a man is dying—"

"Nonsense. He didn't know he was dying."

"I believe he did."

"Even so, I don't attach any special sancity to a deathbed statement. A liar is a liar, under any circumstances."

"I don't believe he was lying."

"It's his word against Mrs. Johnson's. She denies that she gave him any such order."

"Naturally she denies it."

Forest changed his position on the couch, regarding me with a hard and curious eye. "Correct me if I'm wrong. I had a peculiarly vivid impression that you were one of Mrs. Johnson's admirers."

"I am. I'm not sure yet what I admire her for."

He jerked his head impatiently, and rose. "I don't know what you have in mind, Cross. It's just not plausible that any mother would connive at the kidnapping of her own son. You ought to see them together, man. She worships that little kid. She wouldn't let him out of her sight."

"She did yesterday."

"So?"

"I don't pretend to understand this thing. But I'm half inclined to think that Miner is innocent."

"You're crazy with the heat." Forest walked the length of the room and kicked the dead log in the fireplace, violently. He came back, limping slightly, and sat down again: "Forgive the expression, Cross."

"All right."

"I simply meant to say, I think you're dead wrong. Now you may have facts I don't have. If there's any evidence you know of, confirming the dead man's allegation, it would be a good idea to lay it out in plain view."

Two things rose in my mind and dovetailed. Molly had spoken of a red-haired woman who fingered Kerry Snow for the federal men. Seifel claimed that Helen had given him Snow's address in 1946. It would be Molly's word against Helen's. Like an after-image of what I had seen on the terrace, I saw her face threatened by darting, barbed tongues.

Forest was watching me. "Well?"

"I have no evidence."

"Then let's forget it, at least until or unless something does turn up. I don't know how you have this thing figured out. Here's the picture that presents itself to me:

"Miner and Snow were buddies aboard ship. Perhaps they were mutually involved in a racket of some kind—I've never heard of a large Naval vessel that didn't have its rackets. Miner was never caught. Snow was, after the two fell out. Do you know who gave us the information of Snow's whereabouts, when we arrested him in 1946?"

"You told me last night. Larry Seifel."

"He was just the errand-boy. I got it out of him this morning, before they left. Apparently he held back on me because he was afraid of damaging Mrs. Johnson."

"She gave him the information?"

"She passed it on to him, yes, but it didn't originate with her. I questioned her about it. It developed that Miner was her patient at that time, in the San Diego Naval Hospital. It was Miner who gave her Snow's address in the first place. He asked her to turn Snow in without bringing his name into it. Naturally she went to Seifel about it. They were friends, and it was in his line."

"So it all comes back to Miner?"

"You sound disappointed."

"I am. But I'm more relieved."

"It's a rough deal when any man goes rotten," Forest said sententiously. "But everything comes back to Miner, according to my picture. Snow sweated out his years in the pen, and came out looking for Miner. Miner saw him first. He ran Snow down, removed identification, converted himself from a murderer into a hit-run driver. Everybody was taken in except Snow's pal, Arthur Lemp. Lemp may have witnessed the killing.''

"It's possible. I thought of that.''

"But Lemp wasn't the sort of man to go to the police. Not Lemp. We've filled out part of his record, on the basis of the material you dug up, and it goes back a long way. In fact it probably goes back further than we've been able to trace it. He turned up in San Francisco in the early twenties, aged about thirty or so, and got himself a job on the police force. I don't have to tell you the city administration then was sour. Lemp rose to inspector in a very few years but when the city government was reformed—I think it was the third or fourth time it was reformed—Lemp went out. Since then he's scrounged a living at half a dozen trades and petty rackets. He's been arrested for pigeon drop, Mann Act violation, blackmail, and served a total of seven years in Folsom and San Quentin. Blackmail was his specialty, when he could find a victim soft enough—''

"I know enough about Lemp.''

"There's more, plenty more.''

"I don't doubt it. Go on with your reconstruction.''

"Well, he would have liked to blackmail Miner, but Miner lacked the wherewithal. The question for Lemp became: how could his knowledge of Miner's crime be turned into cash? He tried to interest Seifel, without success, or perhaps he was simply trying to pump Seifel for information. In any case, we know the final answer he arrived at. He forced Miner to fall in with his kidnap plans: I maintain that that's the only possible way these things could have happened.''

"It's possible. It leaves out a primary fact, though. Who stabbed Lemp in the neck?''

"It has to be a third party,'' Forest said. "I questioned the boy—he's a smart boy—and he says they drove straight out of town yesterday morning, right after they met you.''

"So that lets Miner out.''

"Yes. It has to be somebody else, somebody who wanted that fifty thousand dollars. Any ideas?"

"Not one."

"I thought perhaps you were going to suggest that Mrs. Johnson stole her own money back." Forest showed his wide white teeth in a grin. "Anyway, we've got the weapon to work on."

Eddied returned from the kitchen, complaining about the lousy telephone-service and the heat. We played three-handed bridge, Eddie winning consistently, until the hearse arrived from Pacific Point. Then Forest turned off the air-conditioner, locked the doors, and handed me the keys.

"Are these symbolic?" I said.

"Maybe they are. Whenever I mention the lady, your eyes glaze, if that's significant. You're just fighting off the idea, old boy. But why fight it?"

His insight was disturbing. I turned away.

The Lincoln led the three-car cortege across the desert, over the snow-blotched pass, down into the green valley. I supposed I was driving it. I hardly remember.

CHAPTER
24

A plainclothesman challenged me at the entrance to the Johnson drive, and let me pass. My car was standing in the turnaround, where I had left it early in the morning. I swung the Lincoln around it and into the garage. As I got out, Helen opened the inside door of the garage. There were shouts and splashes behind her in the pool where the boy was playing.

She looked pleased to see me. Her smile had lost its dangerous brittleness:

"Come in, Mr. Cross. I'm so glad you're safe and sound." I could feel the warmth of her hand through my sleeve. "You'll forgive my running out on you in the desert. I couldn't feel quite secure until I had Jamie home with me."

"You did the wise thing. I notice you have a police guard out front."

"I didn't ask for one, but they thought it best for the present, since there's no man here." She frowned slightly. "Surely nothing else is going to happen to us."

In the green planted enclosure of the patio, it was hard to believe that anything had happened. The flowers in the planters gazed up like innocent eyes into the depthless blue sky. At the shallow end of the pool the boy was frolicking in the water up to his waist, chasing a red plastic beach ball brighter than his hair. There were the remains of a cold lunch on the umbrella table at the far end.

"Isn't he wonderful?" she said. "He hasn't the faintest notion that he was kidnapped, or even that there was anything amiss. The whole thing's been a picnic to Jamie."

"He's been a lucky boy."

Her deep green glance sought mine and held it. "You were his luck, Mr. Cross. I'm grateful to you, forever."

Something inside of me spoke, surprising my consciousness: "I wish he were my boy."

It was the wrong thing to say, and the wrong time to say it. She didn't answer. I turned away. Jamie was jumping up and down in the water, beating its surface with his palms.

"Hi!" he sang out. "I'm a sea-lion. These are my flippers. Where's Fred?"

"He's gone on a trip," I said.

"With Daddy? Did Fred go with Daddy?"

"That's right. They went away together. Fred asked me to say good-bye to you for him."

"Good old Fred," the boy said earnestly. "I'll miss Fred."

His mother spoke softly at my shoulder: "Is he dead, too?" There was a kind of awe in her voice.

"He crashed in the mountains. I was with him when he died."

"It seems so many have died."

"Four men," I said. "Two of them at least were no great loss to anybody."

She made a visible effort to pull herself together, and changed the subject: "You must be tired and hungry, Mr. Cross. Please sit down. Let me give you something to eat."

"I'm tired, but I bet you're tireder."

"Not really. I was on my last legs this morning, I admit. Now that Jamie's back, I feel almost good. Anyway, the sandwiches are already made. Permit me to minister to you with sandwiches. It's the least I can do."

"You're very kind."

I sat by the pool with her and ate her sandwiches and watched her boy and became permeated with a sense of what I had been missing. And would doubtless continue to miss.

"Mrs. Johnson."

She turned her head against the canvas back of her reclining chair. A lock of hair fell forward over one eye. She blew at it, without effect, and laughed. "Lord, I feel lazy." She raised her bare brown arms and stretched, arching her body. "I'd just about dozed off."

"I know you've had your fill of questions today."

"Indeed I have. Did I tell you the reporters were here when I got home? *And* photographers. I want to sink back into anonymity, permanently." She folded her hands in her lap and closed her eyes and smiled.

"Mrs. Johnson."

"I'm listening. You called me Helen last night. I didn't mind."

"Helen, then."

"Your first name is Howard, isn't it?"

"Yes."

She opened her eyes. They were grave. "Hello, Howard."

Jamie was lying face down by the pool, near her feet. He raised his head and echoed her: "Hi, Howard."

"Hi, Jamie."

"Hi, Howard."

I went on in a softer voice, hoping he wouldn't hear me: "Mrs. Johnson—Helen."

"Is something the matter?" She lifted one hand and waved it nervously. "I mean apart from the obvious things, like Abel."

"I've been trying to tell you—well, you know my job. I'm not exactly a cop, but sometimes, in the clutch, I have to act like a cop. There are several questions that need to be answered."

"By me?"

"They concern you."

She sat up, rigid. "Do you suspect me of doing something wrong?"

"It's not a question of suspicion. There are certain facts—"

"You do, then." Her eyes narrowed. "Fire away, Mr. Cross."

The boy looked up: "You called him Howard a minute ago."

"I know I did." She relaxed a little. "Do me a favor, Jamie."

"Go into the house?"

"That's right. I want you to put dry clothes on now. They're on your bed. And don't try to go into Daddy's room. It's locked up."

"Why is it locked up? Daddy isn't in there, is he?"

"No, he's not in there."

She kissed him, suddenly and passionately. He disengaged himself and trotted away, leaving wasp-waisted footprints on the tile.

"I don't know what to tell him," she said.

"Tell him the truth—that your husband died a natural death. That is the truth, isn't it?"

Her face hardened. "Ask Dr. Campbell. Don't ask me. I'm not a physician. I only know what I told you last night. I was quoting Dr. Campbell."

I was off to a bad start, but I blundered on: "You mustn't take offense. I have to ask these questions. Fred Miner said a strange thing this morning, before he died. He said that he was protecting Jamie, that you had ordered him to take Jamie into the desert."

"That *I* had?"

"Yes. I asked him who told him to do it. He answered: 'Mrs. Johnson. She's the boss.'"

"He was lying," she whispered harshly.

"Are you sure?"

She waited a long time before replying. Her oiled face was like a mask gleaming metallically in the sun. "I thought you were my friend."

"I'm trying to be."

"By making covert accusations against me? Is that what you call friendship?"

"I'm sorry. I've got to either clear Miner, or pin the kidnapping on him. I feel an obligation towards the law, the truth, whatever you want to call the abstractions that keep us going, keep us human. There's nothing personal in this."

"Obviously there isn't. I don't suppose you'll take my word that I've done nothing wrong?"

"Not on a blanket denial, no. I'd like something more specific."

"All right then, fire away, and make it fast. I don't want Jamie to hear his mother being cross-questioned."

"You're making it difficult for me."

"I hope so, Mr. Cross. First of all, you'll naturally want to know how long and how well I knew this chap Kerry Snow."

"You've asked the question. Will you answer it?"

"I answered it this morning, to the F.B.I. That tale-bearing little wretch of a Larry Seifel—" She broke off "All I can tell you is the truth. I never heard of Kerry Snow until Fred Miner gave me his name. It was in January 1946

I believe, a Monday morning. Fred was ambulatory by then. He'd had a weekend convalescent leave, and he came back to the hospital in a bad mental condition, at least it seemed so to me. I asked him what the trouble was. He wouldn't tell me, of course—he never has—but he made me promise to do something for him. He gave me this man's name, and his address in Los Angeles, and asked me to pass the information on to the F.B.I. I said I would. All it amounted to was phoning Larry Seifel down at District headquarters."

"Did you know Seifel well?"

"We'd gone dancing a few times. Is it important, in the *abstract?*"

"What about Miner?"

"What about him? He was my patient. I liked him. I always have, until yesterday."

"Did he tell you what Snow was wanted for?"

"I think he mentioned desertion. I got the impression that he'd run across Snow by accident, over the weekend, and recognized him as a wanted man. They served on the same ship, didn't they?"

"Yes. You say you never met Snow, or heard of him before that?"

"I not only say it. It's the truth."

"I believe you."

"You are too kind."

"There's still another point that needs to be cleared up." She sighed. "There would be. But go ahead."

"I'm not sure I can explain it properly. Kerry Snow left a girl behind him, a young creature named Molly Fawn who claims to be his widow."

"Do you distrust all widows?"

"Please," I said. "I'm trying to do my job."

"I'm trying to survive."

"Shall I drop it for now?"

"No, let's get it over with." She smiled bleakly. "You have that abstract gleam in your eyes. Follow the gleam. I can take it, I hope."

"According to Molly Fawn," I said, "Snow spoke of a woman who had betrayed him to the police in 1946. Could you be that woman?"

"I don't see how. How would he know of my part in it?"

"Miner might have told him, or Seifel."

"Why should they?"

"I don't know. I do know this: After Lemp was hired to your husband to . . . observe your movements—"

"To spy on me," she emended.

"Lemp went back to Los Angeles and told Kerry Snow that he had located the woman."

"The woman who had him arrested?"

"Yes. That seems to be what brought Snow here to Pacific Point: the hope of finding the woman and getting back at her in some way."

"And you think I'm that woman?"

"I don't think anything."

"Then why have you been asking me these questions?"

"I was hoping to learn something useful."

"About me?"

"About the case in general. After all, you *are* connected with it. You did have a hand in Kerry Snow's arrest. Your chauffeur murdered Snow."

"It's murder now, is it?"

"Apparently. And your son was kidnapped by Snow's crony."

"Anything else?" she cried, a little wildly.

"Yes, there is one other thing. According to Molly Fawn, the woman Snow was looking for had red hair."

She lay back in her chair like a fighter after a hard round, and spoke with her face averted:

"You disappoint me, Mr. Cross. I gave you credit for some intelligence. If you can't see that I'm an innocent woman, you are a stupid man."

"You're not the red-headed woman in the case, then?"

"I have red hair, I can't deny that. Everything else I deny."

"All right."

"It's not all right. I've tried to be decent all my life. I think I deserve to be trusted. When I learned yesterday that Abel didn't trust me, he lost meaning for me. I no longer cared for him. I feel no sorrow for him."

"I'm sorry," I said. "I suppose I'm oversuspicious. It's an occupational disease in law-enforcement work."

"I'm sorry, too." She would not look at me.

The boy called from the doorway: "Mummy! Is the argument over? I'm ready to come out now."

"Come on, then," she said brightly. "Mr. Cross is just about to leave."

CHAPTER
25

I drove home to my walkup apartment. Emptying the pockets of my trousers, I found that I had kept the keys to the desert house and the keys to the Lincoln. Oddly enough, I liked the idea of having them. I went to bed.

When I woke up there was still light in the window, a sunset light burning like a grate fire behind the Venetian blind. I had been dreaming. I couldn't remember the dream distinctly, but it had left a pattern in my consciousness. An insistent bell had been ringing at the end of the corridor. The corridor was both spatial and temporal. Along its echoing span, a man was running with a boy in his arms. I was the running man, and the boy in my arms was Jamie.

My thoughts were instantaneous, as immediate as sensations. The bell rang again. I reached for the telephone that had awakened me:

"This is Cross."

"Forest. We've traced Arthur Lemp back from San Francisco. Miss Devon thought you'd be interested."

"I'm interested."

"You sound sleepy."

"I just woke up. But I can listen."

"The name he started out with was George Lempke. His father was a German immigrant, an ironworker in Pittsburgh. The son won a college scholarship and worked his way through law school. He was commissioned a second looie in the first war. After the war he practiced in Chicago, and did fairly well for a short while. Then he was caught suborning a witness to perjure himself in a murder trial. He served two years in Joliet, and of course the state association disbarred him. After that he was committed to a mental hospital—"

"A disbarred lawyer?" I said. "Committed to a mental hospital?"

"That's what I said. He must have sprung himself out of it in pretty good time. He showed up in San Francisco in 1922, using the name of Arthur Lemp."

I lost track of what Forest was saying. The dream came flooding back into my mind. The running man was Lemp as well as myself, and boy in his arms with the man's face was Seifel.

"Have you tracked down any of his relatives?"

"Not yet. His parents are dead. He had a wife at one time, but she didn't stay with him long."

"I see."

"Did the D.A. get in touch with you, by the way?"

"What about?"

"He's convening the Grand Jury tomorrow morning. I lit a small fire under him. You're slated to be the first witness."

"All right. Thanks. Good-bye."

I showered and dressed. My hands were overeager. I never did get the collar of my shirt buttoned.

That, and the fact that I hadn't shaved, were the first

things Mrs. Seifel noticed. She came to the door of her suburban ranch-house, faultlessly groomed in a dark silk frock pinched very thin at the waist. Her black eyes examined me thoroughly, and showed no warmth:

"I know you, don't I?"

"We met yesterday. I'm Howard Cross, County Probation Officer."

"I am Florabelle Seifel. If you're looking for Lawrence, he's not here. I don't know whether to expect him for dinner or not, thanks to you."

"Thanks to me?"

"Thanks to your secretary, I should say. It's very apropos that you should come here this evening, I've been wishing to speak to you. This nonsense between my son and your secretary has gone far enough."

"Miss Devon is my assistant, and it's not exactly nonsense. But that's beside the point."

"It's very much *to* the point. You're a public official, and you have some responsibility. It seems to me that your employees should be indoctrinated with some sense of class distinction. I'm not without power in this community, and when I see my son inveigled into a relationship with a social inferior—"

"I didn't come to discuss that with you."

"What then did you come to discuss with me?" She tilted her sleek black head and looked at me with hostility.

Her eyes were hard and black, impervious. It had probably been years since they had seen anything in the outside world that they hadn't wished to see. Her self-assurance was almost paranoiac.

"Your husband, Mrs. Seifel. Mrs. Lempke."

The change in her face was sudden and terrible. The mouth opened, ringed with white teeth, in a silent snarl of pain. The eyes narrowed to glimmering slits. The flesh crumpled. She said in an old hoarse voice:

"Go away. You've only come here to torment me."

"Not at all. I want the truth. I'll keep it to myself if I can."

"I'll kill myself. I can't bear the shame."

"Why not?"

"I can't," she said. "I've made a good life for Lawrence and myself. I refuse to see it end, and go on living."

"It's good for you, perhaps."

"What do you mean by that?"

"Nothing."

She was leaning in the opening, holding herself upright with one hand on the doorknob. The last of the sunset shone on her face like light from a distant fire.

"I suppose you intend to come in," she said.

"It might be more comfortable for both of us."

"Come in then."

The house had an artificial beauty, like its owner. She led me into a glass-sided sitting-room that overlooked a flower garden, almost colorless in the dying light. The white carpet looked as if it had never been violated by a human foot. A Matisse odalisque reclined in an ivory frame above a white chaise longue. The pose that Mrs. Seifel assumed in the chaise was an imitation, conscious or unconscious, of the odalisque's. It added a final touch of unreality.

"Sit down, Mr. Cross," she said wearily. "I understood you to say a moment ago that you intend to keep this matter quiet."

"I will if I can."

"What does that mean?"

"If you or your son are involved in these crimes in any way, obviously the facts have to be brought out."

"Involved in crimes? The very idea is ridiculous, outrageous." She scratched with carmine nails at her throat, the weak spot in her illusion.

"The facts are outrageous," I said.

"Are they not? The most outrageous of all is the fact that you can't get away from the past. It's built into one's life. You can't wall it off or deny it or evade it or undo it. It's inescapably and inevitably there, like a deformed child in a secret room of one's house. How I've paid for my foolishness."

"Foolishness?"

"In marrying George Lempke, against my parents' wishes. I was just twenty, and a very spoiled young girl. I met him at a sorority ball in Champaign. He was handsome and charming—my story is quite banal, isn't it?—and a returned war hero. Any young officer was a war hero in those days, if he had actually crossed the Atlantic Ocean. I fell in love, and married him. A few months after my child was born he was arrested and sent to jail. My father arranged a divorce, and I thought I was rid of George, free to raise my child in peace. But when he was released he found us again. He came to the apartment in my absence and stole Larry from me. They were missing for four days, living in a wretched hotel on the south side. Those were the most dreadful days of my life. My father hired the Pinkerton organization, and finally they caught him. Larry was safe."

"What happened to your husband—your ex-husband?"

"We had him put away. In order to avoid publicity—my father was a leading figure on La Salle Street in those days—father had him committed to a state hospital. Unfortunately they let him go within a year."

"Was he insane?"

"How could there be any question about it? Of course he was insane, criminally insane. A man who would kidnap his own three-year-old son, such a man—" Her voice broke off in a harsh discord. Her hand went to her throat again, kneading the loose flesh between the red-tipped fingers.

"Maybe he simply wanted his son to be with him."

"If he had wanted that, he could and should have led an upright life in the first place. He was unfaithful to me before Larry was born. George Lempke was never anything but an evil man."

"I suppose you know what he did yesterday."

"I know. I realized when Larry described the man he had seen in the mortuary. George came to me back in November you see. Somehow he'd discovered that we were living here and sought us out. I suppose he thought that he could get some money out of me. I told him flatly that if he ever approached me or my son again, I'd have him jailed."

"Does Larry know that?"

"Certainly not. We never discuss his father. I explained the situation to Larry when he was a boy. Neither of us has ever mentioned it since."

"And he doesn't know that the man is his father?"

"Not from me. Can I depend on you not to tell him?"

"It might be good for him to know."

"Good? How could it benefit anyone to rake up those dreadful things?"

"It's on his mind," I said. "He told me about his father yesterday, as much as you'd let him know. I think he may have recognized the dead man, more or less unconsciously."

"Impossible. He was only three when he last saw his father."

"Childhood memories often go back as far as the second year."

"Not Larry's. He has very little recollection of his childhood." She pulled herself upright and leaned towards me tensely. "Mr. Cross, if you have any mercy for a woman who has suffered miserably, you will not tell my son the truth."

"If he asks me for it, I'll tell him."

"No! You'll drive him into insanity if you do, into suicide. He's a sensitive boy. All his life I've had to look after him and protect him."

"How old is he?"

"Thirty-four."

"He's not exactly a boy, Mrs. Seifel. He's a man. If he isn't a man now, he never will be."

"He never will be," she said.

"Not if you have your way."

"How dare you speak to me like that?"

"It isn't kind, I know. But kindness is out of place in some situations. It's possible to kill a man with kindness."

She rose, a dark slim figure against the window. "I'm a

your mercy, of course. I made one serious error thirty-five years ago, and I've been at the world's mercy ever since. I promise you, however, if you do anything to harm my son—I have powerful connections in this country."

"This is where I came in." I got up and moved to the door. "Where is Larry now?"

"I have no idea. Your little blonde person came here about an hour ago—"

"Miss Devon?"

"Is that her name? She literally forced her way into my house. They drove away together in her car."

I found them, still together, at the mortuary. Larry Seifel was standing over the table where the dead man lay. Ann was at his side, her arm around his waist. When they turned to look at me, I saw that both their faces were marked with drying tears. Seifel looked thinner and older.

Ann detached herself from him and crossed the room to me. "You know who he is, Howie?"

"Yes. Does Larry?"

"I told him, just now. I was talking to Mr. Forest this afternoon, and some of the things in Lemp's record—well, they fitted in with other things that Larry had told me about his father."

"How did Larry take it?"

"I don't know. I'm waiting. But I think he already knew. He simply couldn't admit it to himself."

"What do we do now?"

"Nothing now. Please, Howie."

She looked up anxiously into my face. Apparently there was nothing there to worry her. She went back to Larry Seifel. He was gazing down into the dead face, trying to descry the lineaments of the past.

CHAPTER
26

My testimony to the Grand Jury took most of the morning. I expressed my doubts about Fred Miner's guilt, but I didn't say anything about a red-headed woman. She was hearsay evidence, anyway. Molly Fawn was scheduled to testify in the afternoon, and it could wait till then.

From the tenor of the District Attorney's questioning, and the comments of individual jurors, I judged that Miner's guilt was taken for granted. The fact that he had died violently in an attempt to escape seemed to the jury to be proof of his complicity. Because he had been on probation under my supervision, they considered me a prejudiced witness. I was accustomed to that.

When I came out of the jury room, Sam Dressen was waiting for me. His nose was red and his eyes were moist with excitement. Behind him, on a bench against the wall, Amy Miner was sitting with a matron.

The door closed with a shushing sound. Sam grasped my arm.

"Howie, she's run out on us."

I thought for a bad moment that he meant Helen. "Who's run out?"

"Molly Fawn. I left her here with Mrs. Johannes, about an hour ago." He cocked an accusatory thumb at the matron. "The D.A. thought he might have time to put her on this morning after Mrs. Miner. I went downstairs to the office for a while, and when I came up she was gone.''

"It wasn't my fault,'' the matron grumbled. ''My orders were for Amy here. The girl asked permission to go down the hall and wash her hands. I told her to go ahead.''

"What did you think she was doing?'' Sam said. ''Taking a bubble bath?''

"It ain't my responsibility. You didn't say anything to me that she was going to try and run away.''

"I'm no prophet.'' He turned to me anxiously. ''She was as nice as pie out at our place all day yesterday. How could I tell she was going to make a break for it?''

"Take it easy. We'll get her back. If there's any blame passed out, I'll take it. I guess I should have had her held in jail.''

"Sure.'' Amy Miner spoke up bitterly. ''Why don't you put the whole population in jail? That'll solve all your problems for you.''

I looked into her face. Though it still showed grief and strain, she was calmer than she had been Saturday night. Her graying hair had been brushed, and there was a touch of lipstick on her mouth. I recognized for the first time that she had probably been an attractive girl.

"How are you doing, Mrs. Miner?''

"As good as can be expected, after a weekend in your dirty jail.''

"It isn't dirty,'' the matron asserted.

"Okay, so it isn't dirty. I loved it. It was swell. Everything's been swell.'' She raised her heavy brown eyes to my face. ''You saw Fred before he died?''

"I saw him.''

"Did he mention me?''

He hadn't, but I decided to tell the lie. She had been stripped of everything else.

"He sent his love to you.''

"Really?''

"Yes.''

"He sent his love to me?"

"That's what he said."

"Why did he do it? I don't understand."

"Neither do I. I'm sorry."

She said in a low voice: "Everybody's got plenty to be sorry about."

"When are they letting you out of here?"

"Today." But the prospect of freedom didn't seem to cheer her. "The District Attorney promised to let me go after I say my piece to the Grand Jury."

"What are you going to do then?"

"I don't know. Bury Fred. Mrs. Johnson said I can live on in the gatehouse as long as I want. But I'm not staying in this burg, not after all that's happened."

The bailiff opened the door of the jury room and spoke to the matron: "They're ready for Mrs. Miner now."

Sam pulled at my elbow. "We better get moving, eh?"

"Right." We started down the hall towards the sheriff's wing. "How was Molly dressed when she took off?"

"The same dress she had on before, gray cotton, and that brown coat. She had a yellow rayon scarf over her head. My old woman lent it to her to wear."

"Any money?"

"Not that I know of. We treated her to the drive-in movie last night. So this morning she runs out on us, just when we need her. That's gratitude."

"You'd better broadcast a description: Highway Patrol and city police as well as the sheriff's cars. I wouldn't be surprised if she's hitch-hiking north on the highway. Unless she stole a car."

"She'd have no trouble hitch-hiking, not with that figure. What are you going to do, Howie?"

"Sit tight. I had enough running around over the weekend to last me the rest of the year. If you hear anything, call me at my office."

"Will do."

I crossed the street to the small restaurant that subsisted

on the courthouse trade. I felt empty, in more than the physical sense. I had seen and heard a great deal in the last two days, and needed time to absorb the experience. My emotions were in the state of suspension that sometimes precedes a violent change.

The tower clock struck the quarter hour as I stepped up onto the curb. It was a quarter past eleven, too late for morning coffee, too early for lunch. I felt relieved. The courthouse crowd would be after me for a story when they saw me, and I wasn't sure what story I had to tell. I wasn't satisfied with my Grand Jury testimony. I knew what I had seen and heard, the shape and impact of the events. Their meaning still eluded me.

Wondering if Molly had found the meaning and eloped with it, I pushed in the screen door of the restaurant. Its dim brown interior and never-failing odor of cooking grease did nothing to stir my appetite. I sat on a stool at the counter and ordered coffee.

The place was empty, except for a couple in the back booth. Their heads were close together. I recognized them when my eyes became adapted to the dimness: Ann Devon and Larry Seifel.

Ann, who was facing in my direction, saw me at the same moment. She waved and called the length of the room:

"Howie! Come and join us."

Reluctantly, I carried my slopping white mug to their booth. I had no desire to talk to anybody. With what seemed a similar reluctance, Seifel got out of his seat and slid in beside Ann. I sat opposite them.

"What's the good word, children?" I was conscious of a phoniness in my voice.

Ann misinterpreted it. "I'm taking my lunch hour early," she said in some embarrassment. "Larry wanted to talk to me."

"A reasonable wish. He shows good taste." The phoniness was persisting. The scene in the mortuary the night before was too heavy to be pushed out of my mind.

Seifel was pale and tired-looking. He smiled self-consciously, but no charm came. "You don't mind, do you, Cross?"

"Why should I? Ann runs her own schedule."

"I'm afraid you will mind, though, when I tell you what I wanted to talk to her about."

"Try me."

"I've been persuading Ann to leave her job."

"We're going to be married," she said. "Larry just asked me now, and I accepted."

"I hope you'll be happy."

She looked happy. Her face was glowing, and her eyes were bright. She turned to Seifel like a flower to the sun. He was trying hard, but he would never be really happy. He was a self-tormented man, living in the past or for the future, always despising the present that could save him. His present was an aching hollow inside him, yearning like a woman to be filled.

He said through a pained grim: "I have heard heartier congratulations on occasions like this."

"Now you." Ann stroked his arm. "It won't be right away of course, Howie. We'll have time to break in a new assistant for you."

"Have you thought of staying on in the department after your marriage?"

"We thought of it. I'm afraid it's not possible. You see, we're leaving town."

"And going where?"

"Seattle, probably. We both want something different from this place."

"I'll be sorry to see you go."

"So will Mother," Seifel said. "Mother is staying here. I had it out with her last night. We settled a lot of things last night."

Ann lowered her eyes, and smiled to herself.

"I also talked to Forest last night," he said. "About my father. Forest promised to do his best to keep it out of the newspapers. I hope he does, for Mother's sake."

"Not for yours?"

"I don't give a damn. The man was my father. If anybody wants to make anything out of it—"

Ann interceded gently: "Nobody wants to make anything out of it, Larry."

His truculence disappeared suddenly, passing over like a squall. He leaned forward with his elbows on the table, inquiring with boyish earnestness: "Who killed him, Cross? Do you know who killed my father?"

"No. I don't."

"Neither does Forest. He hasn't even a lead. He says the kind of icepick that was used can be bought in hundreds of hardware and grocery stores." A shadow crossed his face. There was malice in it, and a tragic fear. "Do you suppose that Mother—?"

"Certainly not."

"I'm sorry. I know it's ridiculous. I shouldn't have said it. I've been having a bad time with Mother. But she's through running my life for me. I'm going into criminal practice. I'm sick of living on the surface of things. One thing I've got out of this mess: it's brought my life into focus, I hope. I've been playing around, making and spending money, shining up to old ladies—it isn't good enough. You can use life, or you can waste it. I'm going to use it."

"That was quite a speech."

"It wasn't a speech. It's what I'm going to do. I tell you, Cross, life is a serious business."

"I won't argue with that."

His teeth came together with an audible click. The muscles swelled in the corners of his jaws. "There are a lot of things I don't feel like going into. One thing I've got to say. I made a bad mistake yesterday in the desert. I've been thinking about it off and on ever since."

"Stop thinking about it. We all make mistakes."

Ann said: "What are you two talking about now?"

"I told you yesterday, I fired a shot at Miner. If I hadn't, we would have taken him alive."

''Maybe,' I said. ''Maybe Miner is better off dead.'' I finished my coffee and got up. ''Good luck.''

He rose to shake hands with me. Each of us tried to crush the other's hand. Neither of us succeeded.

Ann, who was tipsy on morning coffee and love, called out after me: ''Why don't you get married, Howie? Everybody's doing it.''

I said that I intended to, but not out loud.

CHAPTER
27

My office telephone was ringing when I went in. I got to it before the ringing ended. It was Sam Dressen.

''Have you spotted her?''

''The HP saw her, some time around ten thirty. She was thumbing rides on the highway, a block north of where it crosses Cacique Street.''

''Going which way?''

''North. You were right, Howie. She isn't there now. I checked.''

''They didn't see who picked her up?''

''Naw, they weren't paying any attention. They figured she was a high-school kid or something. Think I should start an all-points?''

''What does the D.A. say? She's his witness.''

''I can't get to him. The jury's still in session, and he's questioning Mrs. Miner.''

''Molly may have simply gone home.''

''Where does she live?''

"Just above Pacific Palisades. I think I'll take a run up there."

"Why don't we both go?"

"Fine. We'll make it faster in one of your cars."

"Be out front in two minutes flat."

Sam had cut his teeth on a steering-wheel and had an intuitive traffic-sense. In spite of the noontime jam in the Long Beach bottleneck, and without benefit of siren, the souped-up sheriff's car took us to the Palisades in a little over an hour. We parked it at a service station a hundred yards beyond the photograph studio.

There was a fire-engine-red convertible standing in front of it. The door of the shop was ajar. In the high sun, the hand-tinted photographs on display in the window wore a hectic flush, like the products of an overenthusiastic undertaker's art.

I left Sam on guard outside and entered the shop as quietly as I could. There were voices in the studio behind the thin-paneled door. I heard a man's voice first, speaking in quick, clipped accents that I didn't recognize immediately:

"Fifty-fifty is the best I could do. I'd be running a very big risk."

And then Molly's voice: "Who isn't running a big risk? My offer is ten thousand, take it or leave it."

"It isn't enough. I'm expected to do all the work."

"What work? I'm putting the finger on her for you. All you got to do is grab the loot. It's like picking a plum off a tree."

"Grand larceny," he said. "A grand larceny tree. I'm sorry, doll. For a measly ten grand, you're going to have to buy yourself another boy."

"Where does the larceny come in? She stole the money. You take it away from her, she can't even raise a squawk."

"How do I know she won't?"

"Because I'm telling you. Because she's as hot as the hinges, hotter than we'll ever be."

"You've told me a lot of tales at one time and another. They averaged out about a fact to a carload."

"This is the straight dope, unless I'm right off the beam." Molly's voice as thinning out under pressure. "She's got the money, she must have. All we do is find out where it is and take it off her."

"All I do, you mean. I should go into the holdup business for ten grand. Even if your dope is straight, which I seriously doubt—"

"Fifteen then. You're the sharpest. I can't handle it myself and I can't take time to argue."

"Twenty-five," he said. "For anything less I can't afford to touch it, believe me, kid. I'm a respectable businessman, remember, I have a lot to lose."

"You're respectable, sure, so what are you worried about. She'd never go near the law. If she did, you're a detective, aren't you? You're only doing your job."

The man's voice came into context. He was Lemp's ex-employer, Molly's ex-admirer, Bourke.

"Uh-uh," he said. "I don't like it. You can't sell it to me for anything less than an even split. For twenty-five, I'll go against my grain and take my chances. Bear in mind that I'm the one with everything to lose."

"What about me? I got my career. If I didn't need a wardrobe for the sake of my career, you don't think I'd be going into this?"

"Twenty-five grand will buy you a lot of draperies."

"Fifteen will buy you Carol back," she said with a flash of spite.

"Twenty-five," he said. "Is it twenty-five?"

"I guess it'll have to be. You always were a dirty gouging chiseler."

"Sticks and stones will break my bones. If I don't look out for myself, nobody else will. R.K.O., kid, let's get down to cases. Where is the *femme?*"

"She's down in Pacific Point. I saw her this morning."

"You're sure it's the same one?"

"I couldn't be wrong. She let her hair grow out, and she's older, but I'd know her anywhere."

"Have you seen her before?"

"I didn't have to. Kerry had this picture of her that he took. He had it with him all through his time in the pen. I found it in the cupboard with his things, after he left. I was going to tear it up."

"What for?"

"She was the one that fingered him way back in '46."

"Is that why you're so eager?"

"Maybe it is, at that. Why should she get away with everything and make money into the bargain?"

"Why should we?" Bourke asked her cheerfully.

"I need the money. I don't know about you, but if anybody ever needed money, I need money."

"Get me the picture," he said. "I'll take it with me. And hurry it up. We don't want to be here when your friends arrive from down south."

I leaned back against the counter, very carefully.

Molly's footsteps receded. A door creaked open. She came back across the room, her feet dragging thoughtfully.

"Hurry it up."

"I am hurrying. Can you imagine Kerry ever falling for her? She hasn't got half my looks."

"You're the best," he said sardonically. "Let me see."

"Don't grab. Even Kerry, with all that talent he had, he couldn't make her look good."

"This is talent?"

"Kerry was very talented and artistic. You wouldn't understand."

"Snap out of it," he said roughly. "Kerry was a bum and you're another."

"Then you're another."

"You may be right at that. Now listen to me. I'm stashing you in a place I know in Venice, a garage apartment off the speedway. Are you set?"

"How do I know you'll ever come back?"

"I'm not that much of a bum. Besides, I got a business I can't leave. How do I know this red-head has the money?"

"Nobody else could have. Only she isn't a red-head any more. She let her hair grown out, I told you. It's gray."

"Where do I look for her?"

"I'll lay it out for you on the way. We better go round by Sepulveda. They're probably watching the highway for me by now."

"If we get stopped, I'm taking you into custody. Understand?"

"Yeah, I understand. They can't do nothing to me. I wasn't under arrest or anything. I'm clean."

"Sure you have that chlorophyll sweetness. I've always loved it in you."

"Go button it where it flaps."

The doorknob rotated, and the door opened inward. Bourke saw me. His hand slid up like a white lizard under his left lapel. I drove my left hand under it, into his body. He swung his left at me, but he was off balance. I brought my right around over his arm, and found his jaw. He looked away to his right in dazed surprise. My left hand met him there.

Bourke went to his knees in the doorway. His head bowed forward in a profound salaam, and bumped the floor. Sam came around from behind me and took the blue revolver out of his hand.

At the back of the cluttered studio, Molly was trying to open the door. The reflection of the sea shone through the curtained windows like a dim blue hope, lighting one side of her face. It was drawn, like carved white bone, and hungry-looking.

The bolt stuck fast in the socket. She never did get the door open.

I left her struggling and chattering in Sam's old arms, and went back to Bourke. He was prone on the floor under the hollow counter. I pulled him up to a sitting position and found the photograph in the breast pocket of his natty checkered jacket. When I released him, he fell back under the counter. He lay gasping for air, his head rolling back and forth like a restless infant's, in months' accumulation of dirt

It was a wallet-sized photograph, tinted amateurishly with oils. The colors were faded, as if long nights of looking had worn them thin. Still I could see the traces of red on the mouth and the high cheekbones, the brownish tinge in the eyes, the coarse henna lights in the hair. Amy Miner.

CHAPTER
28

When we reached the Pacific Point courthouse, Amy had finished proclaiming her innocence to the Grand Jury, and had been released from custody. The D.A. came out of the jury session to talk to me. He felt, and the jurors agreed, that Fred Miner was definitely guilty, but Amy wasn't. I didn't argue. Instead I gave him Molly and the photograph.

According to the bailiff, Amy had walked out of the sheriff's office a free woman shortly before two o'clock. Helen Johnson had called for her in the Lincoln. Presumably Helen had driven Amy home with her.

It was ten minutes after three.

I phoned from Sam Dressen's office. Jamie answered, breathily: "Hi. Is that you, Mummy?"

"This is Howard Cross."

"Hi, Howard. I thought you were my Mummy."

"Where is your Mummy?"

"Oh, she went for a ride, I guess."

"Where to?"

"San Francisco, I guess. My Grandma's here."

The telephone was taken away from him. A woman's voice said sharply, over his protests:

"Who is speaking, please?"

"Howard Cross."

"Oh, yes. Helen has mentioned you. I'm her mother."

"Has she really gone to San Francisco?"

"Of course not. Jamie must have got it mixed up. She's on her way to San Diego with Mrs. Miner. I expect her home early this evening, if you'd like to leave a message."

"Where are they going in San Diego?"

"To Mrs. Miner's family home. Helen insisted on driving her down. I thought myself that it was a case of leaning over backwards—"

"Do you know the address?"

"I'm afraid I don't. They wouldn't be there yet, in any case. They only left a very short time ago." Her voice, which was pleasantly harsh, took on a roguish lilt. "I think Helen expected you to call, Mr. Cross. In case you did, she left a little message for you. She said there were no hard feelings. And may I say for myself, as Jamie's grandmother, I'm looking forward—"

"Thank you." I hung up on her.

Sam, who had his moments, was ready with a San Diego directory. "Do you know her maiden name, Howie?"

"Wolfe. Amy Wolfe." I spelled it out.

There were a number of Wolfes in the directory. We left their names and number in the communications room and took a radio car. The dispatcher reached us by short wave before we passed La Jolla. The one we wanted was Daniel Wolfe, who ran a grocery store in the east end.

Danny's Neighborhood Market was on a corner in a working-class residential district. The store had been built onto the front of an old two-story frame house, so long ago that it was now old itself. On the front window someone had written smearily in soap: *Special—Fresh Ranch Eggs*. There was no sign of Helen's car. Except for a pair of young women wheeling baby carriages half a block away, and an old dog couchant in the road, the street was deserted. The dusty palms that lined it stirred languidly in the late-afternoon breeze.

I left Sam Dressen parked out of sight around the corner. A bell tinkled over the door when I went in. The store was small and badly lit, its air soured with the odor of spilled milk which had long since dried and been forgotten. Behind a meat counter at the rear, a man in a dirty-fronted white apron was waiting on a customer, a young woman wearing tight blue jeans and large earrings.

She asked him for a quarter of a pound of small bologna. He sliced it carefully, weighed it, and wrapped it. His hands were very large, and heavily furred with black hair. The hair on top of his head was thin and gray. His eyebrows were heavy and black. His face looked almost too thin and old to support the eyebrows.

There was a rack of comic books and confession magazines beside the front counter, and I made a pretense of looking them over. The counter was crowded with things for sale: bottle openers and recaps, packages of beef jerky, humorous postcards, rubber lizards, bubble gum, artificial flies imbedded in plastic ice-cubes, cloves of garlic. On the wall behind the counter hung a display card studded with icepicks. The icepicks had red plastic handles.

The man in the apron came forward to the cash register to make change. His customer departed with her bologna.

He leaned forward with one hand on the counter, thrusting one sharp shoulder higher than the other. "You want something?"

"One of those icepicks, behind you."

He turned and plucked one out of the display card. "I better wrap it for you. You wouldn't want to stick yourself."

"I'll take it as it is."

He handed it to me. So far as I could tell, it was identical with the icepick I had found in Lemp's neck.

"They haven't been selling the way the salesman said they were going to sell." His voice was bitter and monotonous, threaded by a disappointed whine. "You never can trust their say-so. I don't think I sold four of them in six months. Anything else?"

"No, thanks."

"That'll be twenty-five cents and one cent tax. Twenty-six cents."

I gave him two dimes and six pennies.

"I can always use the change," he said.

"How's business?"

"It could be better. It could be worse. I can remember times when it has been worse." He slammed the drawer of the cash register. "Don't misunderstand me. I'm not saying the business is good. I got the food plans and the supermarkets to contend with. People I carried on the books for years, they walk right by my store now that they got a little cash money in their pockets." He looked at me with small hot brown eyes. "You on the road?"

"I'm not trying to sell you anything, Mr.—"

"Wolfe. Danny Wolfe."

"My name is Howard Cross."

"You live around here?"

"I'm from Pacific Point."

"You don't say. I got a married daughter lives in Pacific Point. You know her? Amy Miner? She married a fellow name of Miner."

"I know her fairly well."

"You don't say. You should stick around. Amy's on her way down here now. So you're a friend of Amy's."

"I know her husband better."

"Fred?" He leaned forward across the counter, resting his weight on his forearms. "Say, what happened to Fred? I always thought he was a good steady sort of fellow. When he came courting Amy in the first place, I was in favor of him long before she was. She had uppity ideas: an enlisted man in the Navy wasn't good enough for her. Way back when she was a little girl, she had them big ideas of hers. I used to call her the Duchess." He pulled his mind back to the present with an effort. "But it looks like I made a mistake about Fred, after all. He got himself into some pretty bad trouble, I heard. Hit-run driving, wasn't it?"

"He killed a man."

"So I heard. How did he happen to do that, anyway? When Amy came down to visit here this spring, she wouldn't say a word about the accident. When I asked her about it, she flew right off the handle." He scratched the day-old beard on the side of his chin. "I never could get Amy to tell me anything."

"Fred was drunk when it happened."

"You don't say. I haven't seen much of him these last years, but he never went in for drinking when I knew him. Maybe a couple of times he got himself plastered. Mostly it was the other way around. Amy used to gripe about how quiet he was. Course, it was pretty slow for her when he was all those months flat on his back in the hospital."

He glanced up suddenly, his eyelids crinkled under the crushing eyebrows. He was aware of something unspoken between us:

"Say, has Fred had another accident?"

"He was killed yesterday."

"I knew it!" he said in dry self-congratulation. "I knew there was something wrong when I was talking to Amy on the phone. I felt it in my bones. She didn't tell me, but I knew it anyway." Then he sensed his nakedness, and tried to cover it: "It's a dirty shame, I say, a young man like him. Was he drunk again this time?"

"He was sober this time. When did Amy phone you?"

"A couple of hours ago. She said she was coming home. She didn't tell me anything else. She's a secretive girl. She always was a secretive girl. I call it false pride and vanity, if you want my opinion. Amy could never open out to anybody."

"What about Kerry Snow?"

His eyes and mouth grew narrow. He peered anxiously around the store and out to the street. The street was still empty.

"You know Amy pretty well, eh?"

"Better than most people."

"Is Kerry still in California? I haven't seen him in years."

"When did you see him?"

"Back in '45, I guess it was. He used to visit Amy, I guess you know that. I wouldn't want to spread it around unless you already knew it. Amy came home to keep house for me after her mother died and Fred was in the hospital with his back. You know how it is. I couldn't hardly blame her for stepping out a little, and he was a nice-appearing young fellow. You know Kerry?"

"Slightly."

"Then you know what I mean. He's the sort that appeals to women, I never was myself. I told her she was making a fool of herself. He was younger than her, and she was a married woman. I always say a married woman should stick with her first choice. But she went crazy over him, she started blowing all her money on dresses and beauty parlors. Personally I never could see this hair-dyeing stuff. I told her if you're gray, you're gray. I was gray myself before I was twenty-five, and Amy took after me." He patted the top of his head affectionately. "Is Kerry still around in these parts?"

"Permanently."

"You don't say." Wolfe's face struggled with a confusion of vague memories and vaguer hopes. "Maybe with Fred gone, her and Kerry will be getting together."

"I doubt it."

"You never can tell. She was all for ditching Fred and marrying Kerry back in '45." He nudged forward confidentially through the litter on the counter. "They were set to run off together when I put the kibosh on it."

"You put the kibosh on it?"

"Yep." His large hands came together like independent animals, and clasped. "I didn't like the idea of any scandal, understand. Her mother and me had enough trouble with here when she was running around before she married Fred. So I did my duty as a father should. I was father and mother both to her by then." He smiled for the first time, sentimentally. "I dropped a word to the wise, and Fred had it out with her.

I guess he did, anyway. I didn't see any more Kerry Snow around here."

His smile expanded. Then he realized, too late again, that he had given himself away. His smile became a rictus, teeth clenched like an old dog's on the last tearing corner of life.

"Maybe I oughtn't to be talking. Amy goes her way and I go my way. You interested in Amy?"

"Very much."

"Forget I said it, eh? Whatever you do, don't tell Amy what I said. She can be a wildcat when she's mad."

"I know she can."

"You've seen it happen, eh?"

I didn't answer. I was watching the street for Helen. She was a long time coming. The afternoon seemed to be stretching out forever, while Wolfe and I traversed the windy barrens of his mind.

"She'll be along soon," he said. "Don't worry. And you can set your mind at rest about Kerry Snow. There never was anything much between he and Amy. He drove down from L.A. a few times to see her and they went out dancing or to the movies, and that's all there was to it. Ships that pass in the night."

He was watching me closely now, estimating the extent of my gullibility and the degree of my interest in his daughter. The situation had grown unbearable. I terminated it:

"Mr. Wolfe, I'm sorry I have to tell you this. Amy is wanted for grand theft, and on suspicion of murder."

"Suspicion of murder? You're a policeman?"

"There's a policeman outside. I was Fred's probation officer."

"So that's what happened to Fred," he said to himself. 'She killed him, eh? Well, I can't say I'm surprised." His ace was hard and shiny like polished white stone. "I always knew she'd come to no good end. She was defiant. More than once she threatened me with my life."

He turned suddenly, and trotted jerkily to a meatblock behind the rear counter. A large knife flashed like a sword in his uplifted hand. "She threatened me with this here knife! Right here in the store! Her own father!"

"Put the knife down, Mr. Wolfe." Shock had as many manifestations as there were kinds of people, and I didn't want him to cut himself.

He dropped it and came trotting back on stiff knees, his eyes glowing like small brown electric bulbs in his perfectly white face:

"You said grand theft. Did she steal something? What did she steal?"

"A package of money."

"A big package?" His hands outlines a rectangular shape in the air.

"It would be a fair size."

He ducked with mechanical speed and reached under the counter. Now knowing what to expect, I brought the gun out of my jacket pocket.

He came up with a brown paper parcel, which he pushed away from him across the counter as if it were contaminated. "Is this the package you're looking for?"

It bore a yellow express-sticker and was addressed to Mrs. Amy Miner, care of Danny's Neighborhood Market. I broke the string around it and tore it open. Sheaves of fifties tumbled out on the counter-top.

His hands went out to the money. Then he saw my gun and drew back. He wiped his hands on the front of his apron.

"When was this delivered, Mr. Wolfe?"

"This morning. It come by express this morning. I didn't know what was in it. Honest to God, mister. I didn't know what was in it. She had no right to send it here. I never broke the law in my life."

A car door slammed outside. I looked up and saw the Lincoln with Helen at the wheel, and Amy Miner running forward across the sidewalk. She flung the door open. The bell jangled wildly.

"Give me the money," she said. "It's my money. I earned that money."

Her father chattered behind me: "Keep her away. I don't want anything to do with her."

Amy had stopped in the doorway, head thrust forward and elbows high, like a running figure caught in stone. The whole weight of her attention leaned on the gun I was holding. Sam Dressen came up behind her quickly and softly. Blue steel handcuffs glinted in his hand. He circled her leaning body with his arms and snapped the handcuffs on.

She cried out, very loudly: "It isn't fair! It's my money! Thieves! Dirty robbers!"

Later, she said: "I didn't do it for the money. I only did what I had to do all along."

Daniel Wolfe had closed his store for the rest of the day and led us back through it into his living-room. Its blinds were drawn, but some light leaked around them onto yellowing curtains, a worn and dusty carpet, a mohair davenport with balding arms, an old cabinet radio. There were photographs of two women on the radio. One was a wooden-framed studio portrait of a smiling girl in leg-of-mutton sleeves and sailor hat, probably Amy's mother. The other was an enlarged copy of Kerry Snow's photograph of Amy.

Wolfe peered at them through the dim mote-laden air, then sat down with his back to them. The armchair he chose seemed large for him. Tears glittered in the hollows of his face. There were no tears on Amy's face. She sat opposite me on the davenport, with Sam and Helen beside her. A line of light from the window fell slanting across the three of them, touching Helen's head with fire, decorating Sam's blouse with an honorific yellow sash, gleaming dully on the cuffs on Amy's wrists. All the time she was speaking, her hands were pulling back and forth, tugging this way and that against the tightened steel rings.

"They didn't leave me any alternative," she said. "Kerry found me the end of January. This Art Lemp came along with him. Lemp was the one that tipped Kerry off where I was, Lemp had this plan for kidnapping Jamie. Kerry said I had to help them. He said I had to do my part in it to pay him back for all those years in prison. He didn't believe me when I told him that Fred turned him in, that Fred must have followed us to the flat in L.A. that last weekend we had together.

"He wouldn't listen to reason. He was ready to kill me if I didn't help. What could I do? I said that I would go along with their plan. They told me that they would be back the next Saturday for another conference. Lemp called them conferences. All that week my mind was a blank. I couldn't think. I was scared to death that Fred would find out about Kerry coming back. I had this terrible guilty feeling about Kerry. It wasn't the kidnapping plan. That didn't worry me then. I thought it was just a crazy dream they cooked up, that it couldn't work.—It was Kerry. From the first time I saw Kerry Snow, I knew my life would stand or fall with him. It was more than a guilty feeling I had. I felt surrounded, like the things were coming to pass that I knew were coming, way back in '45 when Kerry and me went together, the first time.

"I got Fred drunk that Saturday night. It was his first time in two years, but Fred was always a pushover for liquor. I bought him a bottle myself and fed him a few triples after supper so he wouldn't know what was going on. Then I took the Lincoln and went to meet them at the time they said. It was ten o'clock they said.

"I didn't have any plan to kill Kerry. I wasn't thinking. I just felt surrounded. It happened like automatically when I saw them standing there in the road beside their car, two little men there standing in my lights. Lemp saw me coming and got away. He rolled away under their car. But I knew I hit Kerry. I felt the bumps, double bumps. I didn't care. I loved him so much, but he didn't love me any more.

"I drove up on the ridge away from the city and parked for a while. I tried to think. There was a moon that night. I remember how it looked, shining on the water. It was pretty on the water. I sat there watching it for a while. All I coul think was: 'I killed Kerry tonight, and I'm as cool and calm as moon on the water.' That is the way I felt.

"When I went back, their car was gone. I said to myself: 'I frightened *you* off, Art Lemp. I'm a better man than you are, Art Lemp.' Kerry was lying on the side of the road. He looked dead. He didn't look like Kerry. He looked like a picture of a dead man all black and white in the moonlight. I didn't stop. I didn't want to go near him. That way I could kid myself that he was never alive.

"Fred was fighting blind drunk when I got home. His bottle was gone. He wanted another bottle. I told him he was too far gone to drive, but he wouldn't listen. He was blind drunk and deaf drunk. They picked him up that way in town—I don't know how he ever got as far as town. What could I do? I let him take the blame for what I did to Kerry Snow.

"What else could I do?" she asked us, grinding her bony wrists against the handcuffs. "If I confessed that I was the one, they'd know I did it out of malice and forethought. They'd dig it out all about Kerry and me, how he went over the hill so he could stay with me, and all those days we had in the flat together, and how Fred's jealousy sent him up to the pen. I couldn't tell them. I couldn't tell Fred, either. He could never hold anything back, he always went by the rules. He'd broadcast it to the world.

"Fred never did find out that it was Kerry, and he never did find out that I was the one. I thought for a while, when he got his probation and all, that things would turn out for us yet. Then Art Lemp came back one night. He was scared of me now, I could tell by the way he acted, only he wasn't scared enough. He thought he was smarter than me, that he could outsmart me and out-talk me. I let him think that.

"Lemp told me how lucky I was. He told me he did me a favor, by taking the stuff out of Kerry's clothes so the body couldn't be identified. Now it was my turn to do him a favor, he said. He was full of his plan to take Jamie, still burning up with that plan. He said he was a mastermind, that he could operate by remote control and never get caught.—I was the one that was caught. I had to do what he said, I had to tell him what the Johnsons did at all different times of the day, and spy on Mr. Johnson's savings-book to see how much cash there was. But that last week I worked out a plan of my own.

"He wasn't even going to pay me!" she cried in a surge of anger. "Not a red cent was he going to pay me! A man so cheap, didn't he deserve to die?"

"He deserved to die," I said.

My agreement seemed to calm her. She went on: "And I was the one who had to do his dirty work for him. The hardest part was Saturday morning. I had to lie to Fred and make him believe me. I told him Mrs. Johnson sent him a message, that she was sick in bed and sent him a message through me. She was worried, I told him, because somebody threatened to kidnap Jamie. He was to take Jamie off to the desert house where he would be safe from the kidnappers over the weekend.

"Fred swallowed it. I was glad, not just for myself. I knew the boy would be safe with Fred, as long as Fred had breath in his body. He did take good care of Jamie, didn't he?"

"Better care than he took of himself," I said.

Helen's bright head was bowed forward into her hands.

Amy Miner said: "Fred was always like that. Even after he knew about me and Kerry, he was a kind husband to me. He said that he would give me another chance, and I tried to love him. I tried to be good to him. It's funny, after I killed Kerry Snow, I really did start to love him, but it was too late."

Her father leaned forward. "You ruined Fred."

"Shut up, Danny."

He withdrew his head and neck tortoiselike into the shabby armchair. The time-laden air in the room, cross-sectioned by a single slash of light, was heavy and oppressive. I tried to imagine the childhood that had been passed here, the family life from which Amy had sprung defiantly into the world and fallen beating her angry fists against it.

Helen lifted her face. It was grave and lovely. She said: "Fred Miner was a good man, the decentest man I've known. Thank you for giving him back to us."

"You're thanking me?" Amy said incredulously.

"Just for that one thing, and for caring about what happened to Jamie. I can't forgive you for the rest."

"I didn't ever expect to be forgiven. I didn't hardly expect to come out of it alive. If Fred didn't believe me about the message from you, Lemp was going to make me steal the boy myself. I knew that much. I didn't know all his plans. He was cagy about them. But I caught on fast when I saw that letter he sent you. I said to myself right away: 'Art Lemp, your days are numbered.' " Her voice rang out in the room.

"I had this icepick in the house. I snitched it from Danny's store last time I was down here."

"You always were a snitcher," her father said.

Her mouth twisted scornfully. "Which is worse, a snitcher or a cheapstake? What did you ever give me in my life, except a damn good beating whenever you got the chance?"

"I should have licked you oftener and harder."

"Go on, Mrs. Miner," Sam said.

She drew a deep, sighing breath. "Well, as soon as I could get away, I took the bus into town and went to the station. I could see the front of the newsstand from the window in the ladies' waiting-room. I could see everything that happened: Mr. Johnson leaving the suitcase there, then the bellhop taking it away. I saw Lemp come out of the Pacific Inn with the suitcase, and I followed him down to the beach. It was such a nice bright day. I thought to myself: 'Art Lemp, you've lived long enough. The sun will shine brighter without you.'

"He was trying to start the engine of his car and back out of the sand. I walked right up to the side window. I said: 'Do you need any help, Mr. Lemp?' Before he could answer me or move from his seat I leaned through the window and stabbed him to death. He was surprised. You should have seen his face."

"I saw it, Amy."

"Not when he died, you didn't. I saw him die. He just lay over on the seat and died with his eyes open. It wasn't like killing Kerry when I felt so calm and empty. I was excited. It was what I wanted, to see that old man die."

"No," her father said. "You oughtn't to talk like that. What kind of an impression—?"

"Shut up, Danny."

He fell silent. In the fading light his face was a pair of eyebrows mounted on a white receding blur, his body a pair of thin knees clasped by large hairy hands.

She said: "I was only doing what I had to do, getting rid of him for good and all. It was funny when it turned out that it was what I wanted to do. And then there was the money. I had this wrapping-paper and string I brought from home. I thought if it worked out, if I really had the nerve to kill him, why shouldn't I get the money out of it? Mr. Johnson had plenty left. I never had any money in my life.

"But I couldn't let them catch me with it on me. I took it out of the suitcase and made a parcel out of it and addressed it down here. One thing, I forgot my pen but Lemp had a pen in his pocket. I took the rest of his stuff and buried it in the sand behind the billboard. Then I walked back to the express office and sent off the money to myself. I didn't know they were going to put me in jail. I thought I could get away on Saturday or Sunday and be down here long before the money got here. But first I figured I needed some kind of an alibi. I had to have a reason for being in town Saturday morning."

"So you came to me," I said. "You're a good actress, Amy."

"I always wanted to be one. Only I wasn't putting it on when I talked to you Saturday morning. I was worried about Fred, that they might shoot him. I had to find out how much he said to you. And I knew if he came back before I could get away, and caught on to the lies I told him—Well, I was really worried, and I had a terrible letdown after I killed Art Lemp. The sun wasn't brighter like I thought it was going to be. It was darker. I could hardly see for a while. I guess I would have gone right off my rocker if I hadn't kept holding on to the thought of the money."

Her eyes brooded heavily on the torn parcel lying across my knees. She forced herself to look away from it.

"I'm sorry, Mr. Cross," she said woodenly. "You were a good friend to me, and you were too, Mrs. Johnson. I didn't mean to do bad things to you. I just got caught, through my own fault in the first place. I couldn't see any other way out. Then, when I saw my chance to get that money and keep it for myself—I went for it. That's the whole story."

But she looked around the room as if her story didn't satisfy her, as if its final meaning had been omitted. The room was still and waiting.

"I'll never be anybody now," she said. "They're both dead, Fred and Kerry both. I haven't got anybody left to love me. I'll never get to have a baby of my own."

She had tears left after all. Helen comforted her. Her father watched her from the dim security of the armchair. After a while she ran out of grief, and Sam took her out to the radio car. He was gentle with her, but the handcuffs stayed on.

Helen came up to me on the sidewalk. "Drive me home, Howard, please. I'm afraid I'm exhausted."

"You don't have to say please to me."

"I don't mind saying please to you."

She fumbled in her bag for the car keys.

"I have the other set," I said. "I held on to them yesterday."

"I know you did."

We drove out through the sprawling suburbs, keeping the radio car in sight. The highway gradually curved back to the sea. The sea flowed backward through the rushing twilight like a broad white river on our left.

"I got your message," I said. "No hard feelings?"

"I'm not proud. I can't afford to be proud. I've lost so much."

"I have so much to gain."

"You hurt me yesterday, Howard."

"I was hurt, too. The difference is that it wasn't you who hurt me."

"We'll forget it," she said. "But you mustn't ever mistrust me again."

Her body lay away from me in the seat like a mysterious country I had dreamed of all my life.

"I suppose I should feel guilty about your money and about your husband."

"No. It's entirely my problem. I've been thinking it out."

"Already?"

"We're old enough to tell each other the truth. I fell in love with you yesterday, when we quarreled, when I saw that you were falling in love with me. I gave six years of my life to Abel. I'm being repaid in a way, but it doesn't mean I have to give him all the rest of my life. He lived as he chose, and died as he chose. Most of the money goes into a trust for Jamie, anyway."

"I want the rest of your life. And I don't feel guilty. I never will."

"I'm glad. Of course we'll have to wait."

"I can wait."

Her hand touched my shoulder, lightly.

ABOUT THE AUTHOR

"ROSS MACDONALD" was the pseudonym of Kenneth Millar. Born outside San Francisco in 1915, he grew up in Vancouver, British Columbia. He returned to the U.S. in 1938, earned a Ph.D. at the University of Michigan, served in the Navy during World War II and published his first novel in 1944. He served as president of the Mystery Writers of America and was awarded both the Silver Dagger award by the Crime Writers' Association of Great Britain and the Grand Master Award by the Mystery Writers of America. He was married to the novelist Margaret Millar. He died in 1983.